The shower sounds stopped. Almost breathless, Carly closed her eyes, picturing LauraLee naked and wet. Then LauraLee was standing in front of her, wrapped in a towel, little tendrils of damp hair on her forehead. "Were you falling asleep sitting up?"

Carly swallowed. "My turn?" she asked brightly. LauraLee, her eyes so deep they seemed black, nodded and moved aside so Carly could stand.

Carly took longer than usual in the shower. Her hands were trembling, she kept dropping the tiny bar of soap. Then she bound the towel tightly around her and opened the door. LauraLee was waiting, and Carly walked into her arms.

They kissed for what seemed hours. Pressed together, they breathed into each other, tongues touching. Their movements caused the towels to loosen and slip to the floor. Carly moaned aloud when she felt the pressure of LauraLee's soft naked body . . .

Clearwater

BY CATHERINE ENNIS

Clearwater

BY CATHERINE ENNIS

The Naiad Press, Inc.
1991

Printed in the United States of America on acid-free paper
First Edition

Edited by Katherine V. Forrest
Cover design by Pat Tong and Bonnie Liss
    (Phoenix Graphics)
Typeset by Sandi Stancil

Library of Congress Cataloging-in-Publication Data

Ennis, Catherine, 1937–
    Clearwater / by Catherine Ennis.
        p.   cm.
    ISBN 0-941483-65-7 : $8.95
    I. Title.
PS3555.N6C58   1991
813'.54--dc20

91-25242
CIP

WORKS BY CATHERINE ENNIS

To the Lightning

South of the Line

Clearwater

For Pat and Blackie
From the Beginning

About the Author

A native of Georgia, retired from teaching, Catherine Ennis lives in the south with her lover of seventeen years. In addition to mostly tame cats and dogs, they enjoy the company of assorted small critters that abound in their rural setting. Catherine's hobby list now includes fishing in addition to gardening and cooking. Author of *To the Lightning* and *South of the Line,* this is Catherine's third novel.

Prologue

The young trooper, his arms stretched wide, was herding spectators back behind an imaginary line. "Keep moving . . . Back . . ." He kept his eyes turned away from the car and the other trooper, who was leaning over something just visible on the car seat. "Stay back, please."

This was his first shotgun victim, and the sight of the corpse had caused breakfast to rise to his throat. He was thankful it had stayed there.

He glanced with some curiosity at two troopers questioning a man in a sweatsuit, the runner who had discovered the body. "I run here, same time, every morning." But he had seen no one, heard nothing and was using his towel to dab at the vomit on his shoes.

The street was crowded with cars, and one officer was attempting to keep part of the road clear so that morning traffic could exit the subdivision after he had taken license numbers, names, and addresses.

The trooper leaning into the car straightened, then moved away from the open passenger door, writing something on a note pad. The spectators nearest peered curiously into the opening; peered and gasped and turned away.

The corpse was in the driver's seat, slumped against the wheel, its head more missing than not. The front seat, the headliner and windshield were splattered with gore.

The man with the note pad walked over to the runner. "The police from town will be here in a minute. They'll want to talk to you." He motioned to the curb behind the car. "Why don't you sit there." He looked at his note pad and spoke to the two troopers. "Let's find out if anybody else was up and around last night, probably from midnight on." He thumbed pages. "Marvin Engle, in number eight at the end of the block, heard two backfires around one o'clock. He says it could have been shots, but it was dark outside so he didn't look."

They could hear the sound of sirens coming closer. "That'll be Chief Joiner. Let's clear these people so he'll have a place to park."

Saturday, October 21

The phone rang in the early morning, an hour before I ordinarily get up on a Saturday.

"Damn!" I heard myself sputter as I pulled the sheet over my head. "Damn!"

It rang again, then again.

"Aren't you going to answer it?"

"No," I said from under the sheet.

By the seventh ring, I knew it was no use. I fought loose from the cover and yanked the receiver from the night stand. "Yeah," I growled, "who is this, and do you know what time it is?"

"Bernadette, is that you, my dear?"

I shifted my gaze towards heaven, then sat up on the edge of the bed, my toes touching the carpet. "Aunt Allie? Yes, it's me. What is it, darling? What's wrong?"

"Bernadette, I need you." The voice was tearful. I sat straighter, knowing instantly that there had been a death. For no other reason would Aunt Allie call me at such an ungodly hour.

"What happened? Who's dead?" I am considered to be a woman of few words, and those few words are usually right to the point.

"Albert Junior. He's been murdered." Aunt Allie was a woman of few words, too. "Can you come home?"

I took in a deep breath, thinking of my worthless, and now murdered, cousin. I balanced his death, Aunt Allie's need, the mountains of work to be done before next Saturday, and my absolutely, positively, faithful promise to Vi of an entire weekend at the coast with her. Another deep breath helped me decide that a death in the family, especially a murder, even if it was my least favorite person, was an acceptable excuse.

"Yes, I'll drive over this morning. Tell me what happened."

"When you get here, I can't talk now." Then the line went dead.

I banged the receiver in its cradle. "Damn," I said again, leaning to nuzzle Vi's neck. "Albert Junior is dead. He's been murdered, and Aunt Allie needs me there as soon as I can get moving." My words were muffled as Vi's arms pulled me into a more intimate embrace.

4

"Does that mean you have to leave this minute?" Vivian, not one to fake what she didn't feel, showed neither astonishment nor curiosity, knowing that I positively hated cousin Albert Junior, and cared not a bean that he was dead.

"Is this an invitation?" I settled my weight on her, feeling her warmth through the sheet that was the only thing separating us.

"I can't recall that you've ever needed one." She was smiling.

"You are the horniest woman in the world," I said approvingly, as she pulled the sheet from between us. Then I busied my mouth on her smooth body.

"Ummm," Vi whispered encouragement, "ummm."

I kept to the speed limit crossing the causeway for the north shore, my attention only briefly on the cars and gravel trucks that zoomed past, and hardly at all on the miles of flat, grey water between the north and south shores of Lake Ponchartrain, or the soft music from the new CD that Vi had insisted I take with me. "To keep you from missing me, my dear," she'd said, "although I know music will never take my place."

It was good the bridge was divided into double spans, one for traffic northbound, one heading south for New Orleans, because I kept forgetting that I was driving. The roadway was straight as a stick and, except for tiny mile markers and call boxes, there was nothing to interrupt my thoughts of Clearwater and Aunt Allie and Albert Junior dead. I drove most of the twenty-three miles on automatic pilot.

At breakfast, we'd switched the TV from channel to channel, hoping to hear some mention of the murder, but the only reported overnight killings were those in New Orleans and Baton Rouge. There was nothing in the *Times Picayune* either.

"From the little you've told me, I think it's good riddance. You said he was never up to any good." For Vi, black was black, and white was white. It was only where her lesbianism was concerned that shades of grey were allowed. "I hope you don't get professionally involved, darling, and remember to give my love to Aunt Allie and Cora."

Neither of us had expressed an inch of sorrow for my dead cousin, but Vi's unconcern was simply a reflection of my own attitude. She had never questioned me about Albert Junior, knowing I would speak when I was ready. Vi had no idea why I hated Albert Junior, but she was not preoccupied with every item of my life before we became lovers. In our six years together, she had accepted whatever I wished to tell. "It's what we are to each other that counts," she'd said. And, happier than I ever hoped to be, I agreed.

Ah, well, I thought, as I slowed to exit the bridge, there are six days until Saturday. Maybe that'll be enough for a funeral and whatever else.

It was less than an hour's drive from the lake shore to Clearwater, the quiet university town where Aunt Allie and Uncle Albert had taken me in after the death of my parents in an automobile accident.

6

Photographs from that time show me as an unsmiling, skinny nine-year old, already taller than Aunt Allie.

A mile or two from the lake, I turned west, leaving the interstate system for a state road. It needed repairs but then most secondary roads in Louisiana received scant attention. It was a pleasant drive nonetheless, with tall pines hugging the roadside, and enough small bridges and light curves to keep the greenery from becoming monotonous.

Aunt Allie, tiny, regal, greeted me in the parlor which Cora was layering in black. Aunt Allie's first words were, "Your Uncle Albert is upstairs, resting, dear. This is very hard on him."

"What about you, Auntie?" I said this through clenched teeth, feeling my face redden with the anger which surfaced every time Aunt Allie assumed that Doc's welfare was uppermost in my thoughts. "He was your son, too," I gritted. There was no need to remind Aunt Allie that Albert Junior had been her only child, and I regretted the words once they were out.

Allie Breaux stood as tall as her almost five-foot height would let her and said quietly, "There's no need to bring up unpleasantness at a time like this, Bernadette. What's done is done. Albert Junior is gone from this earth, and you must respect him in memory, if not in life. I require this of you, my dear."

I nodded, my arms reaching to embrace the slight figure who stood rigid before me. I still felt no sorrow for Albert Junior, but tears almost started when Cora embraced the two of us, her arms enfolding, hands patting. "Now, now," she soothed, "Now, now."

Aunt Allie stepped away first. Holding her chin high, she said, "We must talk. There won't be time later, you understand."

While Cora poured hot milk into our cups of thick black coffee, Aunt Allie told me what Doc had told her of the murder. "For that's what it had to be. There is no way Albert Junior could have shot himself dead, then hidden the gun. He was found in an automobile that probably belonged to the used car lot where he worked, because he had sold his car some months ago, and was using theirs. There was no identification on him, so he was not identified until they took him to Albert's clinic this morning. Your Uncle Albert is still our coroner, you know."

"Who did it?"

"Who shot him?" Aunt Allie's hands began shaking so hard that some of the now cream-colored coffee splashed over the sides of her cup. Cora used a cloth to wipe the table, then she put a folded napkin in Aunt Allie's saucer to take up what had spilled. Aunt Allie, holding herself scant inches away from total breakdown, and accustomed to Cora's ministering, had noticed neither the spill nor the wiping-up process.

I looked across the table. Cora, her blue eyes reddened from crying, shook her head just the slightest. So, before Aunt Allie could form an answer, I said, "Never mind all that. You let Cora help you up to bed so you can get some rest, and I'll go down to the station and see what I can find out."

"Would you, my dear? I know you'll be able to find out something . . ." She closed her eyes. My heart broke when I saw tears stream from under her closed lids. I leaned forward and squeezed her hands in both of mine. "I'll take care of things, Auntie, you go rest."

Cora helped Aunt Allie from the chair, walked with her through the breakfast room door. It was only then that I noticed how stooped Cora had become.

Being kin to half the people in town helped me gather facts. I visited for half an hour at the police station. Then my second cousin, Willie, a sergeant on the town's fifteen-man police force, drove me to Hilltop, the subdivision west of town where Albert Junior's body had been found.

The car was there, inside an area circled by barricades and yellow plastic ribbon. Some of the smaller splashes of Albert Junior's head still clung to the car's interior, but the street had been swept clear of shattered glass and Albert Junior's parts.

"We took pictures this morning, but they won't show anything more than what you see here." Willie, massive in his blue uniform, lifted a ribbon so I could stoop under. "There was so many people wandering around it looked like Mardi Gras." He waited patiently as I peered inside the vehicle, first from the driver's side, then the passenger side. "You looking for anything in particular?"

"No," I answered absently, "I don't think so."

"Well, like I said, it looks like the perpetrator was standing on the curb and shot through the open passenger window. They found the door on the curb side wasn't closed tight. Like maybe the perpetrator coulda been in the car first, then got out and leaned back in through the window to do the shooting. 'Course Albert Junior coulda been shot first, then the perpetrator opened the door after, but didn't close it back tight. If he did that, he must of been wearing gloves, because they didn't find any prints —"

I interrupted, "What do you think?"

Willie shook his head slowly, glad to give his considered, experienced opinion. "If the perpetrator was sittin' in the car, I want to know where was the shotgun? Doesn't seem like he'd of leaned it on the outside of the car, does it?" His shrug was eloquent. "Myself, I think Albert Junior sat there, talking to the perpetrator through the passenger window. That way, the per . . ." He grinned when I rolled my eyes skyward. "That way," he corrected, "whoever did it coulda had the gun on the outside, hidden by the car door, then just raised it up when he was ready, leaned it on the door, and blasted away."

Frowning, I worked through what he'd said. "So, the killer came here in a car, parked, walked to Albert Junior's car, poked a shotgun through the open window and pulled the trigger. And, if he parked in back of Albert Junior, it being night and dark, Albert Junior wouldn't necessarily have seen him carrying the gun, would he? Maybe they talked, maybe not."

"Yeah, then he got back in his car and drove off. He wouldn't have to look close to tell Albert Junior was dead."

"Any guess as to the time it happened?"

"There was a light rain close to one o'clock, lasted about half an hour. The street's dry now, but this morning it was still wet, except for under Albert Junior's car. One of the residents said the car wasn't here when they came in from the drive-in around twelve-forty, so that fixes the time between, say, twelve forty-five and one-thirty."

"Then, because of the rain, Albert Junior probably had the windows closed. He opened the passenger window so he could talk to whoever, wouldn't you think?"

"Yeah, it's only the driver's window broken. Makes you think the guy stood outside in the rain, doesn't it?"

"Did anybody hear anything?"

"Nope."

"Willie, I don't think he parked here by accident. Looks like he planned to meet somebody, doesn't it?"

"That's what I think."

"Who was Albert Junior meeting on this street at that hour of the morning? And, why?" I asked this of myself more than of Willie.

"Aw, you know Albert Junior. Who could say what he's up to?"

I ignored his use of the present tense, ducked under the ribbon, saw two women staring at me from the sidewalk. I stared back. "You say the

11

neighborhood was checked again, after Doc identified the body? Nobody here knew Albert Junior? Nobody heard anything, saw anything?"

"Naw. This subdivision hasn't been here but a year or two. All new people. Most work industries on the river, Baton Rouge or so. It doesn't look like anybody here had anything to do with it."

We rode back on the highway that ran through town. I stared out the window, not really seeing what we passed, thinking that the thoroughly despicable Albert Junior had somehow brought his death on himself. I was convinced of it.

As the patrol car stopped in front of the station house, I spoke for the first time. "Do you have any idea why he didn't have identification, a wallet?" I asked. "Could it have been a robbery?"

"Naw, it just doesn't figure that way. None of us think that. Doc asked about it, too, when he opened the clinic to let us put the body inside. None of us knew it was Albert Junior till Doc lifted the sheet." The grimace on Willie's broad face was clear.

"You mean nobody searched his clothes at the scene?"

"Well, yeah, sort of. But Bernie, nobody wanted to touch him. Not to mention going through his pockets. Man, it was bad. You didn't see him!"

I sighed. "No, but I suppose I should. Is his body still at the clinic?"

"I guess so. Doc closed the place, had his nurse cancel appointments for the rest of the day, then he went home after he'd done what he had to do. We haven't heard from him since." Andrew cleared his throat. "We thought we'd wait a while before we called to get his, ah, report. He has papers and things to fill out. For our records, you know."

"He was home, resting, when I got there, but I still know where they hang the key."

"Want me to go with you?"

"No, but thanks."

The lobby where patients waited was the same as I remembered, still smelling of disinfectant and floor wax. The magazines seemed the same, too. I looked around, letting memory take me back. So deep in thought that I jumped when the door next to the nurse's cubicle opened. It was Doc. His fully gray hair was mussed, his shirt open at the collar, and the skin under his dark eyes was red and splotchy.

"I knew you'd come here."

"I thought you were home." I heard accusation and coldness in my tone, even though I hadn't particularly intended it.

"So did Allie." His voice was brusque. "I saw you come in this morning, but I needed to get some things straight in my mind before we talked." He turned. "Come to my office."

I shook my head, saying to his back, "I'm not here to get into an argument." But habit was strong, so I followed him down the corridor, and sat in the chair across from his desk. I waited for him to speak. It took a while.

"He deserved to die, Bernadette, but he was my son and I loved him."

My jaw dropped. That was the last thing in the

world I had ever expected to hear. I didn't know what to say.

Uncle Albert slowly swiveled his chair so that he faced the window, his back to me. I could tell from his voice that he was crying. "I knew something like this would happen someday. He hurt too many people."

Sure, I thought, he hurt me, he hurt Aunt Allie, he even hurt you, but you'd never admit it.

"I want you to find the person who killed my son."

"What?" I leaned forward. "Me, why me?" I asked the back of his chair. "I'm not a cop. Let them handle it."

"No, you're going to do it, Bernadette, but I'll help you." He turned the chair so that we were facing, then pulled tissues from the desk dispenser, blotted his eyes. "I'm going to tell you what I know, what I found, and you'll take it from there."

I shoved back my chair, jerked to my feet. "Nope, I'm not going to take anything anyplace!"

Doc hit the desk with his fist. "Sit down, Bernadette!" We glared at each other, the air almost sparking. Then he said, "Please?"

That did it. I sat.

"I found something this morning in Albert Junior's shirt pocket." Doc handed a piece of paper across the desk. "It's a list of license numbers."

I took the paper but didn't look at it. I shook my head, then placed the paper on the desk and pushed it back to him with one finger. "There's no reason to give this to me. I have no idea what to do with it."

The small piece of paper, a brownish stain covering half of it, lay on the desk between us. It began moving as the ceiling blower caught one raised edge. Slowly, in little jerks, it fluttered back towards me. Doc began smiling and, after a moment, so did I. We watched the paper dance its way to the edge, then I caught it before it fell to the floor.

"Why me?" I asked.

"Because you have easy access to information. We need to know who owns the plates, but if I call it'll be all over the state before I hang up. You know how it is, Bernadette."

I did, indeed, know how it was. "Doc, I'm not a police person. I work in the crime lab, yes, but I don't run around looking for clues or suspects. Things are brought to me for identification, you know that. I work with blood, with hair, tissue, dust, saliva . . ." I paused, knowing it was a waste of time to tell him what he already knew. "I use laboratory instruments, Doc, very highly specialized tools, but I don't question people or make arrests. The police do that."

I looked at the paper in my hand. The stain, I knew, was blood, Albert Junior's blood. The writing was identifiably his, too. I felt excitement, a tiny tingle, causing my heart to beat faster. It came to me then, in a flash, that the numbers, seven in all, were identifiable as local by the Parish alphabet code, and I knew in my bones that the owner of one of them had shot Albert Junior dead.

"I'll do some checking," I said. "See what I can find."

Doc nodded. It would have been the wildest extravagance on his part to acknowledge the truce, the tenuous bond, that had formed between us in those few moments. But he was a grieving father, and thankful for my help, so he said quietly the words that should have been spoken twenty years before: "Bernadette, what else would you have had me do?"

I froze. I had asked myself that question a thousand times, but was no closer to an answer those thousand times than I was now. "I don't know," I choked, "I don't know."

The rest of Saturday was a nightmare. The phone rang constantly as word of Albert Junior's murder spread through the community, and then throughout the state.

Though it had been years since he had left the public eye, Doc was still a well-known personage in Louisiana. He had been Louisiana's "Radio Doc," a call-in health program of the late seventies. He had given advice on the air for everything from taking the pain out of bee stings to handling sprains, burns, poison ivy, fever, diarrhea. The program was directed to the state's huge rural population, people who wouldn't call a medical person if they were dying. They did call Doc, however, and all of them, it seemed, were calling again, but to express sympathy this time.

Aunt Allie answered the first dozen calls, then fled upstairs in tears. Cora, torn between ministering to Aunt Allie and answering the phone, finally set her lips in a straight line. "You answer," she said to me as the ringing began again. "You know what to say."

I did know what to say, and I said it in a few,

direct words. Weary, feeling heavier than lead, I sat at the small telephone desk, leaning on both elbows, head in my hands, jerked into motion when the phone rang, then methodically listing the names of those who called.

Are you on this list, I wondered, knowing that Albert Junior's killer was most likely someone who knew the family, someone whom I, myself, probably had known for years.

Sunday, October 22

For me, Sunday passed as slowly as Saturday, with no letup in the calls. "It's because your uncle knows every person in the state," Aunt Allie told me again, as she looked over the list I had made. "There'll be a few close friends here tonight."

It was a few minutes after nine that night before I could take leave of the gathering in the downstairs parlor. There were no fewer than thirty people, all of them with a favorite Albert Junior story to tell. It was "remember when Albert Junior this, and remember when Albert Junior that" all the way back to his birth, it seemed to me.

I didn't hear anyone mention the cause of Albert Junior's demise. Nor did I hear speculation about who or why . . . either said outright or whispered in the small groups that formed around the room, waiting their turn to participate in the ritualistic solace. These old friends, mostly women, were calling to mind good things about Albert Junior, and I knew this took inventiveness and downright lies. There just wasn't that much good anybody could say about Albert Junior. Doc's influence had kept Albert Junior out of jail a number of times, mostly for stealing something that Doc would gladly have bought for him. To tell the truth, Albert Junior had been on parole of one kind or another for most of his life, and the people in this room knew it.

They weren't exactly standing in line, but they were taking turns capturing Aunt Allie's attention. Aunt Allie, composed, hands clasped tightly in her lap, sat in a wing chair, listening, smiling faintly, but not saying much. Cora, also in black, sat as regal as any queen on the straight chair next to Aunt Allie. Her lips were cemented in a rigid line, her eyes downcast, but she looked up and nodded gravely when anyone spoke directly to her.

I inched my way around people and furniture, until I stood in front of one of the open windows that faced the front of the house. The men, gathered on this wide veranda, were talking, but in tones so low that I couldn't make out any words. Not that I wanted to know. Their subject, I knew from past experience, would be hunting, politics, and the rising interest rate. Not too much about Albert Junior. That would be left for the women.

I held the starched lace aside, hoping for a breeze, thinking that it would take a tornado to clear the fuzz from my brain. I need to talk to Vi, I thought, I really do need to talk to Vi. I had called twice but our machine had answered. I left a message. "It's me," I'd said plaintively. "Where are you?"

Casually, holding the slight smile which I hoped was appropriate, I eased my way around obstructions, and out the parlor's double doors. Then I hurried up the stairs to my room.

Again, Vi didn't answer.

I kicked off my shoes and lay on top of the spread, staring at the ceiling. Finally I closed my eyes, and let my thoughts drift. Images formed and faded, but nothing sharp or clear, just vague outlines like an out-of-focus TV screen. The vision of dead Albert Junior stretched on the clinic's gurney, Albert Junior with a truncated head, was as hazy as the other shapes.

I heard the latch click on the bedroom door and, without looking, knew it was Vi. The faint tinkle of bracelets, the soft rustle of silk, was a clear giveaway. Without opening my eyes I said, "Hi, baby. I'm glad you're here."

Vi sat on the edge of the bed and leaned to kiss me full on the mouth.

* * * * *

For a long time we held each other, listening to car doors slam, the rumble of engines starting. Finally, with Vi nested against me, I began to talk.

"Uncle Albert gave me a page from a spiral binder he found in Albert Junior's shirt pocket. It had license plate numbers on it." I sighed, tightened my arms around Vi's softness. "It looks like Albert Junior was up to his old pastime of blackmail. What he'd do was drive through the parking areas of motels near here, and write down any local numbers. Then he'd call a friend in Baton Rouge to find out who owned the car."

Vi muttered inaudibly, and I laughed. "He'd done this before, years ago when he first came home from LSU. I guess he learned it there, but if he did, it was the only thing he learned. Nobody ever knew how much Albert Junior managed to squeeze that summer before one of his would-be victims beat the shit out of him, and convinced him to give it up. The man was one of Doc's friends. He told Doc that he'd kill Albert Junior if he did anything like that again."

"Did he?"

"Do it again? I guess not. At least I didn't hear any more about it." I had to pause and breathe for a minute, deep in and slow out, to help me collect my thoughts, get things in the right order. "Doc didn't do anything, though. Maybe he lectured Albert Junior about blackmail, but it would've been the same as always. To his way of thinking, Albert Junior could do no wrong. Doc always believed Albert Junior over what anybody else said, no matter what or who." I could hear the bitterness in my tone.

"I think there's more to that statement," Vi said softly. "Shouldn't you tell me now why you hated Albert Junior?"

"Yeah," I said after a few seconds. "Guess so."

Vi waited, knowing I needed to organize my thinking so I could say whatever it was without the embellishment that favored one thought over the other.

"I was thirteen." I tried to keep my voice as flat as a pancake, to not let emotion take over. Vi held very still and kept her mouth shut because, as she said later, she could tell that I was hurting from remembering whatever it was.

"I guess I was pretty stupid for thirteen." I wasn't asking for repudiation, just stating the fact. Vi kept very still.

"What it was . . . was that Albert Junior raped me. And nobody believed me, not Aunt Allie, not Doc, not Cora. I think maybe Aunt Allie and Cora believed me at first, but Albert Junior denied it, and Doc took his part."

Vi snuggled her arm tighter around my waist, but she didn't interrupt.

"I cried a lot. But Albert Junior said he'd kill me if I kept on, so I hushed, except at night in bed. He'd raped me in the car coming home from school, so I pushed the chifforobe in front of my bedroom door every night for as long as he was home. I thought he'd try to do it again."

I heard Vi groan. That same chifforobe was still standing by the doorway — a gargantuan piece of furniture for a frightened young girl to seesaw across the door, night after night.

"Well, after a while I couldn't always eat breakfast. And sometimes I felt funny. Aunt Allie said it was growing pains, but Cora asked me about my period and, wouldn't you know, I was so dumb I didn't have any idea I was pregnant. I didn't really know what pregnant was, or what it took to get that way." Telling had made my eyes brim, the way they always did when I remembered how frightening it had been to tell the truth and have nobody believe me. "Can you imagine anybody being so stupid?"

"No, not stupid," Vi said softly. "If nobody told you, how were you supposed to know?"

"That's what I thought, too." It felt good to tell Vi. She knew I wasn't looking for sympathy. "That's exactly what I asked Cora. I cried and cried because I didn't know what was going to happen and, as big a girl as I was, Cora held me and rocked me on her lap. Then she went to Aunt Allie, and even from upstairs I could hear them shouting. I was scared because they'd never had a fight that I'd heard. That night Doc took me to the clinic, gave me some pills to swallow, and I sort of fell asleep. Next thing I knew, I woke up on the examining table with my legs stretched apart, and Doc poking inside me. I thought he was going to do what Albert Junior did, so I tried to jump off the table, and that's when he hurt me. I remember blood pouring down my legs, Doc chasing me around the room, me crying, him yelling . . ."

Vi raised up to look at me. The memory of betrayal clear, I was really crying now, the tears were streaking my face. I wiped my cheeks with the tip of the sheet. "I guess it was probably my fault. If I hadn't moved . . ."

"Ah, no," Vi breathed. "No, it wasn't."

"Anyway," I said, "I got over it. But I've never trusted Doc since. Funny thing, Aunt Allie thinks I'm a lesbian because of Albert Junior raping me, and what happened afterward with Doc. She isn't thrilled over my lifestyle, but she feels somehow responsible. I think that's why she accepts us being together, she thinks it's her fault for not taking better care of me."

Vi was not at a loss for words. "At least," she murmured, "justice has finally prevailed. For the rest of his life, dear Uncle Albert has to bear the thought of Albert Junior's head being blown to the four winds."

We considered that for a while. It did seem fitting.

My tears had stopped. I said, "You can imagine how I felt when Doc asked me to help find the person who killed Albert Junior."

"Are you going to do it?"

"Vi, honey, I don't really care who killed him. Whoever did it probably had a damn good reason, and I'll stand in line to pin the medal."

"What about the police? Won't they be looking, too? After all, murder is murder, even if it's deserved."

I thought for a long time about what she said. "Vi, they'll look, but what can they look for? I doubt if the police will find any fingerprints. There are no footprints, no tire prints, no gun, nothing to help identify anybody. Remember, I have the list of license plates that Albert Junior had in his pocket. I don't think Uncle Albert made a copy, so, without knowing why Albert Junior was killed, where are the police going to look?"

"All that may be true, my love, but you didn't answer my question. I still want to know if you're going to try."

"You know I am. It's just that I don't know how I'll feel when, or if, I learn who did it. I would have killed him myself years ago, if I'd had the means."

"Hush, you couldn't kill anybody."

I turned so that we were front to front, and I touched my lips to Vi's. A sweet, gentle kiss. "I needed for you to be here," I whispered, my breath caressing her face. "I'm so glad you came."

"Well," Vi said pragmatically, "there's a nut running loose with a gun, and I knew you'd be in the middle of it. I had to come take care of you."

Vi and I met at a summer pops concert in New Orleans. I was looking at my program, not paying attention to the people who were still being seated. I heard, "May I pass, my dear?" and, my eyes still on the program, I nodded and turned my knees to the left. After a few seconds, when nothing happened, I looked up and saw a woman leaning on crutches, waiting. I mumbled apologies, and stood so that the woman could maneuver past. Then I had to wait for the woman's companion to struggle over the crutches which had somehow become wedged under the seat in front of me.

Once the three of us were settled, I went back to

my program, but I remained aware of the woman next to me.

"It was your perfume," I'd say to Vi later. "That, and your jewelry tinkling every time you moved. I don't know what I listened to most, you or the concert."

Thinking about that night always made me laugh. "You kept rubbing my arm with your elbow," I'd insist, "and I thought you were wearing bells." I always swore that Vi made the first move, but Vi recalled it differently.

"Ah, no, my dear. It didn't take a Philadelphia lawyer to figure out what you were up to, even though we blessed your kindness in offering us a ride, what with the rain starting, and me with a broken foot. Recall, if you will, that Agnes' old car was dead in the street, and no cabs in sight. Remember also that I lived in the Quarter, not five blocks in a straight line from the auditorium, and Agnes lived out by the lake. I don't know what possessed you to take Agnes home first."

I would revel in my own cleverness, and grin hugely at Vi's next words.

"You almost flew Agnes home, you devil, then took an hour and a half to get me back to town."

"Well, of course," I'd say, smugly. "I had to get rid of Agnes. She outweighed me."

I fell in love with Vi that very night. I was relieved to learn that Agnes was simply a friend from the lakefront university, and had been kind enough to act as chauffeur because Vi couldn't drive with a cast on her foot.

Vi made it perfectly clear that she was not "encumbered" in any way, so I began courting her with single-minded purpose. Together, we attended each of the remaining concerts, Vi now actually and purposefully rubbing her arm against mine, to the point that we often left before intermission, racing to Vi's apartment, and the delights we had discovered in each other . . .

Monday, October 23

Doc and Aunt Allie had gone to the funeral parlor by the time we came downstairs in the morning. Vi sighed with relief when she saw only two places set at the table. I was having serious second thoughts about what Doc had asked me to do, and Vi knew from my morose expression that one wrong word from Doc would have escalated into a verbal battle. For all our sakes, Vi wanted that open confrontation to be avoided.

Cora, her white hair in a neat bun, had my eggs crackling in the skillet before we'd unfolded our napkins. "Here," she said as she served my plate, "just the way you like them."

I concentrated on swirling the yolks into a mound of steaming, yellow grits. Ignoring Vi's horrified expression, I cut a thick slice of ham into generous chunks, then stirred them into the mixture so that they settled like pink islands in a saffron sea.

"You'll weigh a thousand pounds before you're thirty-five, and your cholesterol count will be higher than your weight if you keep eating like that." Vi, sipping unsweetened coffee, took a dainty bite of dry wheat toast. "Cora, you're going to kill this woman. I spend my every minute trying to keep her healthy, and you destroy her with one meal. We'll need a hoist to get her out of the chair."

Unconcerned, I floated a spoonful of Cora's homemade strawberry jam in the well of butter that soaked my first biscuit, then took a huge bite, washing it down with cafe-au-lait.

Cora merely smiled and shook her head. Obviously, it made her feel good to have me at the table again. According to her, neither Allie nor Doc ate as much as they should, and Cora liked for people to eat. "Honey," she said to me, "after breakfast, I'm going to bake you a pecan pie."

Vi groaned and pushed back her chair. "I give up," she said, "I can't watch any more of this. I'm going upstairs to put on my face." Bracelets tinkling, she stalked out of the breakfast room.

I had started to say that the face Vi was wearing looked perfectly good the way it was, but I knew that Vi was giving me time to be alone with Cora. I put down my fork. "Okay, Cora, what's going on? What happened?"

Cora's blue eyes widened. "I don't know, baby. I don't know any more than you do."

"Cora," I said quietly, "don't give me that." Thirty-five years with the Breaux family might have whitened her hair and wrinkled her brow, but she was still the one person who always knew what was being done, when, and by whom.

"This time it's true," she said flatly. "You knew Albert Junior moved out two months ago? Well, what you maybe didn't know was he and Doc had a big fight. About some drugs Doc said Albert Junior had stolen from the clinic. Actually, Doc kicked him out." Cora grinned across the table. "Never thought I'd live to see anything like it."

"Was Albert Junior on drugs?"

"He was." Cora's compressed lips showed her displeasure. "He made out like he was selling cars, but nobody sells cars in the middle of the night. All hours, day and night. It was killing your aunt."

"What else was he doing? How did he live?"

"Nothing else that I knew of. He may have gotten money from your aunt. I know she gave him money all the time."

"You know who killed him?"

Cora shook her head, her eyes wide and innocent.

"Doc asked me to see what I can find out. Where do you think I should start?"

Cora was surprised by my question — it showed in her face. After a moment she said, "Don't ask me, 'cause I don't know." She pointed to my plate. "Aren't you going to finish?"

"I can't eat another bite, honest. Vi keeps me on such short rations that my stomach's shrunk. But I'll have room for pie this afternoon."

* * * * *

I didn't have anything to say on the way to
Baton Rouge. Vi looked at the pines on her side of
the road for a while, then she turned and watched
me. She could tell I was stewing, and needed to get
what was bothering me out in the open so we could
talk about it; she also knew that I first liked to
gnaw at problems in private. But, after what I'd told
her last night, I knew she felt that private was not
the way to handle things this time. She studied my
profile, I tried to erase my frown, neither of us
spoke. Obviously, at this rate, we'd get all the way
to Baton Rouge without a word being said, and
words needed to be said.

"If you'd been my little girl, I wouldn't have let
that happen to you."

I chewed my lip for a moment, then snorted.
"You're too young to be my mother. Anyway,
contrary to Aunt Allie's thinking, it wasn't her fault.
Nobody let it happen. I don't know why it still
bothers me so much, it was so damn long ago."

I slowed behind a truck towing a trailer full of
used tires. "What's bothering me more is why I
agreed to stick my nose in this. Doc and I have
hardly spoken to each other for twenty years." I
made a fist and pounded the wheel to emphasize my
next words. "Damn it, Vi, he manipulated me like I
was five years old."

I felt my face flush with anger, my knuckles
showing white as I clenched the wheel. Cursing
under my breath, I swerved the car to the left, and
stomped the accelerator, passing the truck with a
burst of speed.

31

Vi had told me that long after I had fallen asleep last night, she had lain awake, unable to quiet her thoughts. She understood that Doc had maneuvered me into an almost impossible position; I was damned if I did, and damned if I didn't. It was not fair, of course, but fairness didn't enter into it.

"I know why you're sticking your nose in it," Vi said. "Because Aunt Allie asked you for help."

I snorted again. "Yeah, but I actually wasn't going to do anything. I didn't intend to go looking for a murderer, that's for sure. I went to the police station, I visited the crime scene, and I looked at what was left of Albert Junior. And, really, that's all I planned to do."

Vi sniffed, and I darted a quick glance at her, marveling at the crown of fine, dark curls that framed her slender face, the flawless complexion, her slightly upturned nose. "Vi," I asked, "why, if I wouldn't turn detective for Aunt Allie, am I doing it for Doc?"

"I can think of one reason, my love." Vi was choosing her words carefully. "There's a slim chance that Doc really does think Albert Junior's death was deserved, but he doesn't want Aunt Allie to learn what Albert Junior was up to that was so bad someone would blow off his head because of it. If the police solve the murder, the sordid details will be spread over every parish in the state. That would break Aunt Allie's heart."

I nodded. "I guess we both want to protect Aunt Allie, I'll give Doc that much."

"Well, I'm giving him the benefit of the doubt." Vi took a deep breath. "Honey, there may be a couple of other reasons Doc pressured you into this. Have you thought about revenge?"

Puzzled, I shook my head.

She hesitated, then said, "Well, this may be far-fetched . . . but what if Doc doesn't want the authorities to know the killer's identity because he wants to exact revenge without drawing suspicion?"

"What?" I barked.

"Look at it this way. If some person not apparently connected to Doc, or Albert Junior, or the murder, gets killed, who's to say Doc had a part in it? Don't you see, if he had no apparent motive, Doc could commit the perfect crime."

I thought about that for a minute, then shook my head. "You're way off base. Doc wouldn't do anything like that."

Vi sniffed. "I think your precious Doc will do anything he feels like doing. And that could even include a little blackmail." Vi reached to touch my arm. "You, my darling, discover the killer. Then, to protect your aunt, you tell only your loving uncle and he, in turn, whips up a little blackmail of his own."

"Aw, Vi, that's crazy."

"Maybe, maybe not. At least it's food for thought."

Again, we rode in silence, Vi's hand now resting on my thigh. It occurred to me that both Vi and Doc knew I'd do my darndest to protect Aunt Allie. What Doc may have forgotten was that I was not good at deception. I could keep a secret, but . . . conceal a killer, even for Aunt Allie?

The highway was becoming crowded as we neared

the city. I kept to the speed limit, for once not minding the eighteen-wheelers that roared past, their wake causing my small car to shudder.

"You're upset about something else, aren't you?"

"Are you reading my mind again?"

"Well," Vi drawled, "I recall the ease with which I read your one-track mind the night we met, my dear, and I've had plenty of practice since. So let's have it."

"It's Cora."

Astonished, Vi repeated, "Cora?"

"Uh huh. She lied to me about Albert Junior."

"What did she lie about? I thought you and Cora were as close as twins."

"We are. That's what bothers me. She told me he was into drugs, and then denied he could have been doing anything else. Like blackmail." I gnawed my lip. "You see, she wouldn't have done anything about it, or said anything to anybody necessarily, but she would have known. Cora always knows everything that goes on, especially when it's Albert Junior's stuff. She knew him like the back of her hand."

"What did she say that was a lie?"

"It's not exactly what she said. It's more what she didn't say. See, I'm pretty sure that Albert Junior was blackmailing somebody, or trying to, and Doc knows it, too. But when I asked Cora if Albert Junior was up to something more than drugs, she said she didn't know of anything. I don't believe her."

"Honey, why would Cora lie to you?"

"I don't know, I simply don't know."

* * * * *

As we neared the city I turned onto the interstate, the fastest way to the other side of town where most of the state office buildings were located. We rode above the local traffic for a mile or so, then I pulled off to find a service station with a pay phone so I could call a friend at the DMV. I read the seven numbers to her, then walked back to the car. "She'll have a printout ready by the time we get there. Then we can go shopping, if you like."

"Ah, my dear, when did I ever refuse to shop?"

"Never, that I know of. Want to go to a mall?"

Vi thought for a moment. "Let's go to the mall that has a bath shop. I'm thinking of having the bathroom at the coast painted. What do you think of blue and white?"

I eased the car back into traffic. "Blue and white what?" I teased, good humor restored now that the first move had actually been made. "Stripes or spots?"

Vi did the driving back to Clearwater, with me slumped in the passenger seat gnawing my thumbnail and reading and re-reading the computer printout from the DMV.

Vi kept silent as long as she could. "Well," she finally urged, "what do you see?"

"Nothing I want to see, I'll tell you that." I folded the paper, making a tube which I began to slap against my palm.

Vi sighed. "Are you going to tell me, or are you going to drum on your own flesh for the rest of the afternoon?"

I shook my head. "I have a problem."

"I know you have a problem, my dear, but that tapping isn't going to solve it. You'll feel much better if you let me in on it."

Carefully I unfolded the paper, straightening it on my lap. "Some of these people I know," I began, pointing to one of the names. "Like this one, Sidney Bodman. He's gay. Everybody in the world knows it, and he doesn't care. He lives with his mother but he takes his occasional boyfriend to a motel because his mother would die if he carried on in her house. In every way he's a perfectly respectable citizen. He's in every civic club, goes to church every Sunday, gives to all the charities . . . every everything. He owns the paint store on Front Street, has for twenty-five years." I was shaking my head.

"I take it you don't think he's a candidate for blackmail?"

"He doesn't have anything hidden to get blackmailed about. He'd laugh in your face if you even suggested it."

"Well, then, cross him off the list."

I stared at the paper, tapped it with my finger. "Look here, this is Mrs. Vaughan's car. She's eighty-two or eighty-three, and I know she wasn't slipping into a motel to meet a lover." I smoothed the paper with my palms. "What this is, I think, is her family using her car because they can't stay with her in the nursing home. They fly into New Orleans once every year, take the bus here, then stay in a motel and use her car to get around. She can't drive anymore, see, but she won't give up her car." I sighed.

"If that's so, cross her out, too."

At this moment, it seemed the list just might not represent what Doc and I thought it did. The license numbers may have had something to do with Albert Junior's job at the used car lot. If it did, this would make it easier on me. And Vi approved of everything that kept additional stress from me.

"Vi, this thing is making me sick." I folded the page, began tapping again.

"What's making you sick?" Vi guided the car around a travel-trailer. "Please stop that drumming."

"There's somebody on here I don't want to think about." I paused. "Not as a suspect, anyway."

"Who?"

"My first love, that's who." I turned sideways so I could look at Vi. "Her name is Carly Harrell. She was my high school chemistry teacher, and I was in love with her for years. Unrequited, of course, but I loved her with such a passion that just saying her name almost turns me on right now."

This was quite an admission, coming from someone who hardly ever talked about herself. Vi saw that I wasn't smiling, so she kept her attention on the road and said, "Tell me about this teacher of yours."

"Yeah, well . . ." I had to collect my thoughts, and it took a minute. "I always wanted to touch her. I thought if I could just touch her hand I'd be happy." My sigh was deep. "She was the most beautiful person I'd ever seen, and I dreamed about her for the longest time. Years, actually." Another sigh. "She was married, of course, and young. Maybe eight or nine years my senior. She had a child the year I was a sophomore, and I baby-sat a couple of times in the summer, just so I could be in her house, sit where she sat . . . well, you know how crushes are."

Vi nodded. Yes, Vi knew how crushes were.

"I never, ever, worked so hard in any class, before or after. I made straight A's in chemistry so she'd notice me. It did make her aware of me, I'm sure, but she was a teacher, and if she knew how I felt, she didn't let on. She did say once that she was proud of me, and I floated on air for weeks." I unfolded the paper, then re-folded it, creasing the folds with my thumbnail.

"Could she have been . . . one of us, do you think?"

"Naw, no way. I'd have known."

"What ever happened?"

"Nothing. I graduated, went away to school, and haven't seen her since. Years ago, Aunt Allie told me that Carly's husband and little boy were killed in a boating accident. I called several times, but she didn't answer my messages. So I gave up."

Vi, who always claimed that my tenacity was legendary, now said, "I can't imagine you giving up on anything, my dear."

Reaching to pat her arm, I said, "Well . . ." I couldn't help but grin. "I met you, and you were busy seducing me, so I kind of let it slide. But she could have reached me if she'd wanted."

"But now her name is on your list?"

"Big as day."

"What are you going to do? You have to check her out, don't you? And the others?"

"Vi, I really don't think I want to."

"But you will." Vi watched me fold the paper into

an even smaller piece. Then I nodded. Being me, I would.

Because of all the cars in the driveway, Vi had to park on the street in front of the house.

"How long can you stay?" I had forgotten to ask Vi, what with everything happening.

"Until next Sunday, if necessary. My choral group has practice all this week, but they'll live without me this once. Someone in the department will take that over, and Agnes will cover my classes. But I have a staff meeting Wednesday, so I'll drive to New Orleans then take the bus back here so we can drive home together." She smiled as my face lit up.

"Vi, those are the sweetest words of tongue or pen. I really need you here, you know. What I have to do this afternoon," I said, "is get in touch with a friend of mine. It won't do for me to do any snooping around, because everybody knows me. My poking into things would be a dead giveaway that I know something the rest don't know."

"Is there any way I can help, my dear?"

"Well, Aunt Allie didn't say, but I know she'll ask you to play the organ at the funeral home. You will, won't you?"

"Certainly." We were at the front door. Vi waited for me to open it, but it opened before I could touch the handle.

Doc stood in the opening. Hardly noticing Vi, he growled, "You've been to Baton Rouge?"

Later, Vi agreed that Doc couldn't have made a

bigger mistake if he'd planned it for weeks. I heard her draw a breath, waiting for the explosion. It came within seconds.

I snarled, "None of your damn business where I've been. And if you can't find some manners, the next place I'm going is *home!*"

I shouted the last word, and we could hear it echoing in the hall behind Doc's back. Vi reached for my arm, determined to yank me out of harm's way. Doc was a head taller and sixty pounds heavier, an unfair advantage even if I was younger and a skilled karate practitioner.

Doc's neck began to swell, his eyes bulged, his hands clenched and unclenched. In those few moments, I realized that it wasn't Doc's rudeness that had brought my feelings into the open, it was twenty years of hurt. Vi tightened her grip, fingers digging into my flesh.

Then it was over. Doc exhaled, and his whole form shrank like a punctured balloon. I saw the dark circles under his eyes, the deep lines etched from nose to chin, the sprinkle of white stubble on his cheeks and jaw. His face looked like an unmade bed. He closed his eyes for a second, then he looked at Vi. "Of course," he said. "Thank you for coming, Vi, and welcome to our home. Please, forgive my rudeness." He held out his hand. It looked dry and thin and without strength.

This has broken him, I thought. He's a broken old man. Vi's eyes had narrowed, and I could almost read her mind. *I feel pity for you, Doc,* her look said, *but don't you hurt my Bernie.*

For a moment Vi was caught between us, one hand clutching my arm, the other hand held by Doc.

Vi didn't want to let go of me, and it seemed that Doc had gone into a trance, so we stood unmoving for the space of several breaths.

"Vi, dear, we didn't have time to greet you properly last night, but we're very pleased that you could be here. How long can you stay?" Aunt Allie took no notice of me or of Doc. She took Vi's hand and guided her through the hall to the parlor opening. "I want you to meet some very old friends," she said pleasantly.

Vi put on her company smile, and walked into the parlor with Allie at her side.

Still standing in the doorway, I said to Doc, "I shouldn't yell that way, I'll be hoarse for a month." It was as close to an apology as I wanted to get.

In the late afternoon, after the house cleared of visitors, the four of us ate sandwiches in the breakfast room. Cora, who had been on her feet since early morning, insisted on serving. "This'll be your supper, and it's all you're going to get, so eat up. I know it's not what you're used to, but I've been busy trying to make ready for after the funeral." She walked around the table, adding ice to the glasses.

Vi paused between bites. "Make what ready after, Cora?" she asked.

Allie answered. "Our friends will bring prepared dishes . . . meat, vegetables, desserts . . . before the funeral, then come here from the cemetery and eat what they've brought. Custom has the immediate family staying the night at the funeral parlor, but

41

we decided not to do that." Doc's grunt gave the reason they were not going to do that.

"Isn't that hard on the family?" This was Vi's first funeral in the deep South.

"Maybe," I said, "but that never stopped me from eating some of the best dessert I've ever tasted. When I was a kid, I looked forward to funerals so I could pig out."

"Bernadette!"

I grinned at Aunt Allie. "It's true, isn't it, Cora?"

"Huh," Cora laughed. "There isn't anything I wouldn't put past you. You were the snippiest little girl I ever saw."

"You don't go to Carl's house on Monday, do you Cora?" Doc spoke for the first time.

"Doc, you know I don't. All these years I never have. Shellie fixes for him on Monday, because I do our wash here every Monday."

"Then you haven't heard?"

"Heard what? I haven't heard anything for two days. Do you know what it is to get this house clean for company? I don't even talk on the phone, I'm that busy."

"Carl's in the hospital, Cora. He's had a stroke."

Cora's mouth flew open, and she sat down hard on a kitchen chair. Ice slopped out of the pitcher, and slid across the floor.

We shoved back chairs, bumping into each other trying to reach her. I grabbed the pitcher before it fell and slammed it on the counter, then I turned to Cora but Aunt Allie and Doc were leaning over her, Doc holding her hands, Aunt Allie her shoulders. Doc asked, "Cora? You all right, Cora?"

Cora was stricken. She began rocking back and

forth, moaning. Aunt Allie told me to get a damp cloth, but Vi had already dampened a napkin. Gently, Allie wiped Cora's forehead.

"Is Mr. Carl dying?" Cora, recovering, pushed all the hands away.

Doc sat back down. "Yes, he may die." After a pause, he added, "But we can't predict the ultimate outcome."

"What's that mean?" Cora asked.

Doc shrugged. "His age and general state of health are against him. It's been over forty-eight hours since he was admitted and, well, the prognosis isn't good. There's a high mortality rate with this kind of stroke, but we're doing what we can, Cora."

I appreciated that Doc didn't talk down to Cora, or give her reason to hope when there probably wasn't any. In his attitude I saw genuine concern, both for Cora, and for his patient.

"Does that mean he can't walk or talk or anything?"

"That's right." Doc nodded.

"Poor Carly," Aunt Allie said. "She must be devastated."

Vi's eyes questioned. Carly was a rather unusual name for a female. Was this the Carly that I once loved? "Who's Carl?" she asked in a whisper.

"The Carly we talked about," I said, "he's her father."

"Will you play for us, dear?" Aunt Allie asked.

We were dressed to go to the wake, waiting for Doc to return from the hospital. It was already dark.

The piano, huge and ebony-black took up two-thirds of the room. It had always intimidated me, but Vi, sitting on the padded bench, her hands poised above the gleaming keyboard, looked as if she and the monster had been made for each other; they fit as if they'd been designed as one piece.

"What would you like to hear?" Vi would be familiar with whatever Allie requested. Vi was a musical genius.

While Allie was deciding, I slipped out of the room. Upstairs, I sat on the edge of the bed, thumbed through my address book, dialed, then counted rings. He answered on the fifth.

"I need to know where certain people were at a certain time. You interested?

He didn't ask who was calling, he knew my voice. He merely said, "How soon?"

"Right away," I answered. He grunted, so I said, "At least tomorrow."

"How many people? Where are they located?"

"Seven. They all live in Winston or Clearwater, and I don't think any of them strayed very far. This is personal, Donald. Personal and private."

"Can't do it in one day by myself. It'll take two, three more agents, maybe. It depends."

"Get as much help as you need, but no one," I repeated, "no one must know."

"Right. Read off the names, Bernie."

I read names and addresses from the computer print-out. I told him what I needed to know, and why I wanted it. Donald had been my father's partner, now retired, an ex-cop doing private work, and I knew I could trust him with my life. I gave him the information I had on Bodman and Vaughan.

"Call me as soon as you have anything. And, Donald, it's probably a good idea to dig around for anything unusual, you know the routine." I gave him my number. "Call me as soon as you have anything interesting."

I sat, looking at nothing, my hands quiet in my lap. I was listening to the soft melody that Vi was playing. The music made me think about Carly Harrell. When we were entering Clearwater this afternoon I had seen Carly's picture smiling at me from a political poster. The confrontation with Doc had wiped it from my mind. But now I remembered.

The funeral home, a converted ante-bellum mansion, huge and white, was crowded when we arrived around six o'clock. Twenty people, at least, stood on the veranda, and Doc greeted them with a nod. The funeral director met us at the open doors. He shook hands with Doc, embraced Allie, quietly greeted Vi, Cora, and me. "We're in the front parlor, Doc," he said in a hushed tone.

Doc and Allie leading, we entered a vast, carpeted hall. Towards the middle, on the left, was an arched opening, flanked on both sides by arrangements of tall white gladiolus. An ornate pillar to the right of the opening held the book which visitors signed. Bronze letters on a black background spelled out *Albert Forbes Breaux, Junior.* Organ music, with just a breath of static, filled the room.

Allie, clinging to Doc's arm, turned to Vi. "I've made arrangements for you to play the organ. Mr. Turner will show you." Her chin high, she walked through the opening, past friends and relatives, her eyes on the closed coffin at the far end of the room. We followed, a step or two behind.

"Looks like the whole town's turning out," I murmured to Vi. "They're here because of Doc and Aunt Allie, not because they cared about Albert Junior." Vi and I soon drifted to the back of the room, avoiding the crush around Doc and Allie. Cora, seated in the family area with them, held her mouth in a grim, unwavering line. For some reason, a trick of perspective perhaps, Cora seemed much smaller to me. "She's sort of hunched, older than she was earlier, don't you think?"

"Well," Vi answered sympathetically, "she did practically raise him. There has to be some feeling, wouldn't you say?"

I leaned over and whispered, "I'd say my feeling is that somebody in this house, somebody here right now, killed the bastard. You know, Vi, if nothing comes of those numbers, I'm not going to snoop around anymore. I don't care what Doc says."

"I hope you mean that."

"Of course I mean it."

"Ma'am, if you're ready?" The funeral director led Vi out the door. In a few minutes the music crackled to a stop then Vi began playing *Amazing Grace*, Aunt Allie's favorite. The sound was soft and beautiful, and a lump formed in my throat.

I had intended to stay in the background, properly solemn, ready to greet my near and distant relatives, and my friends, as they appeared before me; I refused to be an active participant in the funeral ritual, which I considered unnecessary. But it was not to be. Doc came for me. "Your Aunt wants you, Bernadette." So I followed him, took the seat next to Allie, and held Allie's hand.

I could see that Doc kept his gaze focused everywhere but on the coffin, which was of dull grey metal, adorned with goldtone hinges and handles. There were flowers, a white *prie-dieu,* and a floor length, pleated curtain concealing the scissored cart with wheels on which the coffin rested. To me, the whole thing resembled a freight car waiting on a side track.

I let my mind fill with Vi's music and blanked out what everybody was saying about Albert Junior. Wakes are barbaric, I thought. I'm not going to have a wake when I die. I sat as long as I could, idly surveying the mountains of flowers banked around the coffin and spilling over into what I could see of the next room.

"I'll be back in a minute, Aunt," I whispered, intending to find Vi, keep her company for a while.

I walked slowly, keeping my gaze focused on the carpet, trying to avoid eye contact with someone who'd feel it proper to stop me in order to talk forever about the "dear departed" Albert Junior. I was not surprised when a hand touched my arm as I turned in to the hall.

"It's Bernadette, isn't it? Bernadette Evangeline Hebert."

The voice was unmistakable. It was low and soft and smooth and warm. I had dreamed that voice for years, had dreamed that hand, too. I lifted my head and looked straight into Carly Harrell's gray eyes and, for a moment, lost the power of speech.

Carly was smiling her beautiful smile. "You're Doctor Hebert now, I hear."

"Uh huh." I had done my best to answer, but I was sixteen again, and my beloved teacher was standing very, very close. My throat clamped shut tighter than the grey coffin. I could not say what it was that I felt, but, whatever it was, it was overwhelming, and breathtaking, and powerful.

"I was very pleased when I heard, but you were the smartest pupil I ever had, so I wasn't surprised." She took her fingers from my arm, but I could still feel heat, and the gentle pressure. "It's good to see you, even under these circumstances."

"You, ah . . ." I cleared my throat, blurted, "You're running for office. I saw a poster . . ."

"Yes. Mayor. I'm trying to give Roger a run for his money, but I had no idea that campaigning was so intricate. Not as complicated as your work, however. You're still with the crime lab in New Orleans, aren't you?"

I was puzzled, but immensely pleased. My voice showed signs of returning. "How did you know that?"

"I read the article about you in the *Picayune*. It was in our Sunday edition, and I saved your picture."

"You did?" My mind flashed to the high school yearbooks I'd bought, year after year, simply because Carly Harrell's picture was in them.

"Of course. I'm proud of you, Bernadette. I think I told you that long ago."

"You did. Yes. You did. I remember." And I had lived on those few words for the longest time.

She said, "I should talk with Allie and Doc for a minute. You weren't leaving, were you?"

"No, I came with them. We'll be here until the

parlor closes at ten, I suppose." I paused, said, "I heard your father was ill. How is he?"

Carly shook her head. "They tell me he won't recover, it's just a matter of waiting. My sister is with him now. We both felt that one of us should make an appearance here. We've known Allie and Doc since we were children, you know, and I had Albert Junior in my very first class." Carly hesitated. "Have they learned who killed him? I've been so busy with Pop that I haven't seen a paper."

"Not that I know of. I suppose that'll be a matter of time, too." We were about the same height, but Carly was softer, thinner, infinitely more delicate. "I was sorry to hear about your father," I said, wondering if Carly had been there the night Albert Junior had been blown away. Had she done the blowing, perhaps? I could not believe that she had.

"I want to pay my respects, but I'd like to talk with you. Would you mind waiting?"

I had managed to gather my wits. "No problem, Carly, I don't mind at all, because there's someone I'd like you to meet." The "Carly" came out of my mouth smoother than a duck slides into water.

The last time I had seen this woman, the afternoon of high school commencement, I had called her "Mrs. Harrell," had thanked her for her encouragement, the letters of personal commendation she'd written, and whatever else young Bernadette Evangeline Hebert could think of, so that I could stand close. A dozen other graduates were waiting for their moment, so I finally turned away. I should have been happy on that special day, but I wasn't. I'd felt hollow, empty.

At the time, I did not understand the feeling that held me. Soon, however, in a third floor apartment, on the coldest night of my first year in college, with a female professor, I learned. And, as in most things, I learned very fast.

On that night, as orgasm followed orgasm, it was not to my discredit that I cried out, "Carly!" And again, "Carly!"

"What is it, darling, you look so strange." Vi's hands kept moving on the organ, but her focus turned to me. "You look like the proverbial cat, the one with mouse on its breath. What happened?"

"She's here, Vi. We've talked. She didn't do it. I know she didn't. Really she didn't."

Vi knew the "she" of my reference. "I need a break. You wait."

Vi's fingers were touching the correct keys, but all of her concentration was now centered on other than the keyboard. The music swelled, softly died; Vi pushed a few buttons, the music started again, then she turned to me. "Is she as marvelous as your memory of her?" There was no one else in the room so Vi could be direct.

I didn't answer her question. Instead, I said, "I want you to meet her."

Vi sat very still for a moment, then looked down at her hands. "Bernie, should I worry?" she asked softly.

"I'm not going to dignify that with an answer. Come on."

* * * * *

I watched Carly walk towards us. She was very attractive — this could not be denied. She was, perhaps, every bit as wonderful as the mental picture I had painted. Vi darted a glance at me, and saw my grin stretching from ear to ear. I was highly amused, but Vi couldn't know why, or at what.

Carly was an inch or two taller than Vi — almost exactly my height. She wore glasses, and was beginning to gray at the temples. Vi was not graying yet, although both women were about the same age.

I guided them to a small alcove under the spiral stairway, then said quietly, so as not to be overheard, "Carly, this is my lover, Vivian Barr." Vi's look at me was totally unbelieving. Then I said, "Vi, meet Carly Harrell, my first love."

Both women were speechless. For a second, Carly looked as if she'd gone into shock, then I saw a tiny smile flicker at the corner of her lips. Carly and Vi stared, open-mouthed, at one another, then they both looked at me.

Amusement still high, I said, "I had such a crush on you, Carly, that it almost killed me. I wonder, did you know?"

Carly laughed quite openly. Her laughter was as soft and smooth and warm as her voice. She took both of my hands in hers, and held them. Then she looked at Vi, and shook her head in amazement. "Has she always been like this? If so, I don't remember." Squeezing my hands, she said, "Of course I knew, Bernadette. How could I not have known? You practically climbed all over me at every opportunity." To Vi she added, "Teachers contend with crushes all the time. Most young girls get over it when they find boys are more interesting." She shrugged. "Some don't, however." My outrageous introduction apparently hadn't fazed her. Give her credit for that, I thought.

"Well, I'm glad I didn't. Get over it, I mean." My look at Vi was intended to make the reason for being glad perfectly clear. I saw that Vi was holding her breath, probably wondering how outrageously far I intended to go. I withdrew my hands from Carly's grip. "You're like us now, aren't you. How long have you been out?"

Vi was dumbfounded. She knew I was straightforward, but had never known me to ask personal, embarrassing, questions.

Carly's composure slipped a notch. She sputtered, "How . . . what makes you say that?" I saw fear, quickly hidden.

"I can tell," I said easily. "They say it takes one to know one." I was highly pleased. "Carly, would it be all right if I called you? After the funeral, maybe? I'd like for us to get together." I was usually not this forward, either. It was a day of surprises all around.

Carly hesitated, but only for an instant. "It would be fine, Bernadette."

We came back early from the wake. Aunt Allie had started weeping; nothing anyone said could stem the tears, so Doc had brought her home. Cora put her to bed, then sat in a rocker by the bedside, waiting for Allie to fall asleep. Doc wandered through the downstairs rooms, called the hospital, spoke with the on-duty nurse, then finally sat on the veranda with a glass of bourbon and water as company. Vi and I got ready for bed.

"Where are my bottoms?" Clad only in my pajama top, I was brushing my teeth.

"I have them."

I grinned at myself in the mirror. I knew the meaning of that. I rinsed my mouth, patted my face dry and stalked into the bedroom. "Reading my mind again?"

"Not quite, my dear. I wanted to get your attention in the most direct way I knew. We have talking to do, Bernie. Later, if you like, we'll think of other things." Vi was pillowed against the oak headboard, the covers pulled waist high. She patted the bed. "Come sit here."

Still grinning hugely, I settled myself, facing Vi.

"You've been full of yourself all evening, Bernie, and I want to know why." Before I could answer, she added, "You were shockingly rude, and that's not like you at all. In fact, I've never known you to embarrass anyone deliberately, the way you did today. I wouldn't have been surprised if your Carly had slapped the hell out of you. I think she showed amazing control —"

I interrupted. "She's an in-control lady, that's why. Anyway, I knew she wouldn't."

"You've suddenly turned psychic?"

"Well, sort of." I became serious. "It didn't take me two seconds to become absolutely certain that she was a 'committee member.' She may always have been, just not acted on her feelings, but I knew beyond any reasonable doubt that she's sleeping with a woman now. I don't know if I smelled it, or felt it, or saw it in her eyes, but it was a feeling I picked up the first minute I saw her. I could tell she was in love, Vi, because she was glowing."

"Remarkable."

"Carly's remarkable?"

"No, you're remarkable, my dear. And you're courageous, too. I don't think I'd have had the nerve to blurt it out like that."

"Aw, I don't have that much nerve, I just remember how honest she is. Once she knew the truth about us, why would she be upset if we knew about her? Anyway, knowing that about her helped me figure out why her license number was on Albert Junior's list."

"Well, why?"

"It's like this: one, Carly is running for public office, which makes her vulnerable. Two, she faces a serious dilemma because she lives in the house with her father, and she's sleeping with a woman, not an easy combination. Three, Carly has to take her lover to a motel, or the lover takes Carly . . . whichever. Anyway, four, they're being cozy in a motel room on the night Albert Junior makes his rounds. And, five, Albert Junior takes down her license number, and now has ammunition for blackmail." I yawned. "See how simple? Once I knew the way Carly was leaning . . . well, everything else fell into place, and I knew why her license number was on the list."

"Not everything. You said she didn't shoot Albert Junior. What does your marvelous intuition have to say about that? If she didn't kill him, and I don't think she did, then who's responsible for his death?"

For me, the answer was still very simple. "Somebody else, that's who. I'm convinced blackmail was the reason he was killed — by somebody who had more reason than Carly, who had opportunity, who had a weapon, and the guts to use it."

"Bernie, you've given Carly enough reason to kill ten people. Not that she did, but people have been killed for less reason."

"Sure. We had one murder that took place over a thirteen-cent shoelace. But honey, Albert Junior's murder was planned. It was an execution. There were two shots, the second one unnecessary. One shot was certainly enough."

"You've been patting yourself on the back all evening, but suppose you've guessed wrong and Carly's lover turns out to be a man? You could be left with a mouth full of foot."

"My dear Vi, if I had been wrong she could have denied it and stomped off. She didn't. Anyway, have I ever been wrong? About anything?"

Vi laughed and pulled me to her. "Know what I think? You should warn your darling Carly about meeting her lover in a motel. When they tryst, they should pick someplace less public. We always went to my apartment, remember?"

"You're wrong. I remember motels all over the place. Weren't we the two women who didn't leave a certain hotel room for three days? Sent out for food? Didn't wear a stitch except when the food came?"

"That was different. At least we had the good sense to go out of town."

"Vi," I said patiently, "they probably were out of town. In Winston, would be my guess. Anyway, she's not my darling."

"I'm certainly glad about that. I like Carly." Vi tightened her arms. "But I was slightly jealous, can you believe it?"

"No, I can't." I touched my cheek to Vi's. "I did love her once, I can't deny that. But it was puppy love. It was not, and is not, the kind of love I have for you. You're my beloved. It's you I want . . . always."

Vi sighed, content. "Do you want your bottoms?" she asked softly.

"No."

Tuesday, October 24

I would have grumbled all the way to the cemetery, except that I was riding in the family limousine. Aunt Allie stared straight ahead at nothing, her hands knotting a black handkerchief; Doc stared out the window; Cora and Vi, sitting on the jump seats, stared at the driver's back; and I glared at my shoes. I will not have a wake, I was thinking, I will not even have a funeral. I will be cremated, and my ashes can be put in a flower pot as fertilizer. I will not subject anyone to the barbarism of a funeral.

It had been an unremarkable funeral, as funerals go. There was a crowd, yes, and some slight confusion as to which car belonged where in the procession, but Vi's music had made it bearable for me. Aunt Allie was, once more, in control, and was doing fine until the coffin was wheeled out. Then she had collapsed; she simply fell to the floor in a faint. Because this was not an unusual occurrence in a funeral parlor, smelling salts were instantly at hand. Allie was revived, and managed to walk on her own to the limousine. Doc was not quite steady on his feet, but I attributed much of his hesitancy to the bourbon and water which he had drunk for breakfast.

It was soon finished. Albert Junior was laid to rest, the mourners returned to their cars, and the family settled into the limousine which drove us all home.

Cora went directly to the kitchen, changed from black to white, and put on an apron. With the help of her two nieces, she began setting out the food.

Vi went upstairs to cry. I followed, holding her as she sobbed. My tears were very close to surfacing, too.

"I can't stand it, Bernie. Allie doesn't need a thousand people lounging all over the place. Why doesn't she send them home?"

"It's custom, darling. It's expected of her, and Aunt Allie is a stickler for doing the right thing. This part will be over soon."

Allie and Doc finally bid farewell to the last of the mourners, then Allie retired upstairs, and Doc went to the hospital. Cora finished in the kitchen, sent her helpers home, sat rocking in her room. Vi and I shared the porch swing, each of us with a glass of tea. We weren't talking, just swinging slowly, sipping occasionally. Vi asked what I was thinking, and I said, "I'm just watching the grass grow, my love."

I had the cordless phone beside me on the swing, so I could answer before Allie was disturbed. It rang. I growled "Hello," then didn't speak for some minutes. "Yeah," I finally said, "Thanks, friend. This was personal, so send the bill to me."

I pushed the off switch. "That was Donald," I finally said. "Damn!"

Vi waited, knowing from my expression that he hadn't uncovered anything.

I put my glass on the floor and turned to Vi. "Sidney Bodman was home with his mother Friday night because his car was in the garage on Front Street with a broken water pump. He didn't leave the house, unless he rode a bicycle, and he doesn't own a bicycle. Mrs. Vaughan was in the nursing home, and she didn't leave her room all night. Now, get this. Carly was in New Orleans Friday night and most of Saturday. She had a motel room on Tulane Avenue, and she wasn't alone. See, I told you Carly didn't have anything to do with Albert Junior's murder."

"And you were right, of course. But what about the others on the list?"

"Donald said essentially the same thing about the other names. Their whereabouts can all be accounted for at the time Albert Junior was shot. Donald wanted to get the information fast, so he assigned one investigator to each person." I shook my head in amazement. "Vi, there isn't anything hidden that can't be found out if you know how to look, and Donald's people know how to look. They even checked out family members who might have been involved. It just doesn't look as if anyone on the list blew Albert Junior away, even if they had a reason."

"So it's a dead end?"

"It is, if I'm to believe Donald. And I believe Donald."

"Then we can go home in the morning?"

"Let's stay another day or so, okay? In the morning, you go in to your meeting, come back on the bus. Then, if Aunt Allie is all right, and after I've talked with Doc, we'll leave together Thursday morning, and drive straight to the coast."

Wednesday, October 25

Vi left soon after breakfast. She touched my hand before opening her car door. "I think you should call Carly this morning. If she has some free time, get together and make friends."

I watched Vi's car swing around the corner, then out of sight. Slowly, I walked back up the driveway to the house. As I climbed the stairs to the side door, I told myself that I would like to be friends with Carly Harrell. Yes, I'd really like to be her friend. Then, following my biological inclination, I wondered if I'd like to be more. I thought of touching her, holding her. I thought of taking her to my bed, now that I knew what to do. To any bed. I saw myself making love to Carly, her avid response. I imagined stroking her soft, inner thighs. Doing more.

By the time I reached the top of the steps, I was more than a little aroused. The feeling held until I walked through my bedroom door, and breathed in the faint scent which had always identified Vi. I sat on the edge of the bed, my hand resting on the telephone, and remembered last night, our whispered lovemaking, our hushed laughter as the bedsprings echoed every movement, my own helpless cry as Vi's fingers and mouth brought me to a shuddering climax.

Ah, no. Nice to think about Carly. Nice, but no.

I dialed the number Carly had given me yesterday. She was home, she would like to see me. Could I come over now?

Carly was waiting; she opened the door before I rang. "Come in, Bernadette. It's good to see you."

She led the way through the front part of the house to the sun porch. I sat on a wicker lounge, Carly on a matching rocker. For a moment, we simply looked at each other. Carly broke the silence. "Would you like some tea?" She paused, smiling. "But I have cold beer, if you'd prefer."

"Sure," I said ungraciously, "beer's fine." Something was happening to my voice again. Maybe beer would help.

I heard the refrigerator door close, then Carly

was back with a tall glass full of dark liquid, topped off with just a tiny bit of foam. Not being a regular beer drinker, I had forgotten that the small, local brewery thought bitter was best, and proved it with every bottle. I took a huge mouthful. Then, with limited success, I tried to control my astonishment when the liquid threatened to triple in volume before I could swallow. Beer foamed out of my mouth and nose, splotching my shirt and slacks, spattering clear across to Carly's shoes. When I could catch my breath, I said unhappily, "This is a great way to get to know each other again. I usually have better manners."

Carly nodded sympathetically. "That beer does take getting used to. You're nervous, I think. But then so am I, Bernadette."

"You?"

"Why, of course." She went into the kitchen, returned with a cloth. My clothing had already absorbed the icy brown liquid, so I gestured towards her feet. "Better wipe your shoes," I said, "or it'll look like you're wearing dalmatians."

She dismissed my witticism with the faintest of smiles, eager to get to whatever it was she wanted to impart. "It's what you said yesterday, Bernadette, at the funeral parlor. I'm not accustomed to having anyone reveal her personal life so openly."

I had the feeling that another shoe was poised to drop.

Carly frowned, her gray eyes darkening. "That's not why I wanted to talk with you, Bernadette."

The "Bernadette" was beginning to get to me. Except for Aunt Allie and Doc, I hadn't been called by all three syllables in years. Judging from the seriousness of Carly's expression, this wasn't the time to protest, so, very carefully, I asked, "Why did you want to see me, Carly?"

"I'm being blackmailed."

If I hadn't strangled before, this would have caused it. "Who?" I blurted, although I knew very well.

"I don't know. The voice was disguised." Carly said this very simply, as if I should have known without asking. "He threatened to expose me and . . . someone else. Said he had pictures, although I don't know how that could be."

I got right to the point. "Have you been to the police?"

"No. I don't know what to do, Bernadette. I want to win the mayor's race. It's less than a month until elections, and so many people have spent so much time on my campaign that I simply can't withdraw. What reason could I give?" She shook her head. "I won't use Pop's illness as an excuse."

"Carly, I appreciate your confidence, but why are you telling me?"

"Because," Carly said reasonably, "you're the only one I know who has had experience with crime and criminals. You're the only person who would . . ." She paused.

I gulped, the bitter taste making my eyes brim. What should I say to her? I was so certain that Albert Junior was the blackmailer that I knew I could end her torment with a few words. But, what if I was wrong?

"Tell me what to do. Tell me how to deal with blackmail." Carly's eyes were haunted. "He called Friday, said he'd call again to let me know how much money he wanted, and where to bring it. But that was five days ago, and he hasn't called back. I have lived in absolute terror since then. I know if I give him money I've only touched the tip of the iceberg. He'll have a hold on me for the rest of my life, won't he?"

I knew she was stating the obvious, not making a query, so I asked, "Does anyone know?"

"No. Except for you, I haven't told a soul."

I stared down at my hands, reached for the beer, raised the glass to my lips, thought better of it, put the glass back on the table, cleared my throat, looked through the expanse of window which faced me, idly noted that the huge live oak was crowned with moss, and made a decision.

"He has pictures, you say?" There had been no pictures, not in Albert Junior's car, nor in his shabby room. Were pictures out there somewhere?

"Yes, but I don't know of what. I've been very discrete." Her gaze focused on the wall behind me; her faint flush told me she was remembering what she had done that required discretion.

"And I'm sure you were." My smile was meant to be supportive, encouraging. Still, her posture remained rigid. She was sitting forward, grasping the arms of her chair, knuckles straining, her expression now one of expectancy; the ball was in my court.

"Yes," she agreed faintly, "we were very careful." Then her voice became hopeful. "It's possible, I suppose, that he's lying. I can't imagine when, or better yet, *how* he took pictures of us, or what, exactly, he photographed. We certainly gave no one reason to chase us with a camera."

"How long have you . . ." I asked this because it

seemed to me that in all probability she had been sending signals since day one.

"You mean when did we give someone a reason to take pictures? I don't know which . . ." Carly pressed her lips together, looked away from me. ". . . which night." She leaned back in the chair. "Why don't I tell you from the beginning? There may be something, some pattern that's obvious to everyone but me. I have to go back to last August . . .

"My sister, Shellie, and a local group called Women for a Better Government, urged me to run for mayor against the incumbent. Their reasons for choosing me aren't relevant. But I felt pushed because they wanted a commitment. You see, Pop had been ill for some time, unable to work on any kind of schedule, so I'd been running his insurance business in addition to overseeing the real estate office. I'm not an accountant-type person, Bernadette, and there seemed to be so much haggling that I was almost out of my mind.

"Pop's illness was one reason for my reluctance, but there were others. There were also reasons why I felt I should give it a try. One very sleepless night I made my decision . . ."

August Three Months Earlier

The sign above the door said Whitt, Inc., Real Estate and Insurance, and underneath in smaller print, Notary. Large mullioned windows flanked the glass door, and green plants lined the inside sills. Inside, a woman sat on the edge of a desk, cup in one hand and a telephone receiver in the other. Carly waved and went in. "Phyllis, why are you here at this hour? It's way too early for you."

"I have a client hot for that highway property and I've been up since the crack of dawn trying to get everybody together at the same time. We're meeting at nine." Already moving toward the door, she looked at her watch. "I'm late."

Carly waited for her to leave, then turned the brass bolt to lock the door.

The large room was a pleasant place in which the agents could work and meet clients. Carly had decorated it in soft, autumn shades, adding numbered festival prints to the walls, each poster bright with color and motion. The office furniture reflected softly in the polished pine of the original flooring.

With some trepidation, she had had the paneled ceiling torn out and the original tin ceiling restored, adding three feet to the room's height and allowing installation of old-fashioned, hanging glass fixtures. Carly enjoyed the room's soft warmth, and felt that an increase in sales had been the result of the casual, comfortable atmosphere.

At the far end of the room there were stairs, but Carly ignored them, opening a door to reveal the cage of a freight elevator, its age not in the least disguised by a fresh coat of paint and carpeted floor. She yanked a dangling rope, starting a noisy motor housed in the third-floor attic. The elevator began a lurching ascent.

The day had not started, yet she was already tired with the thought of eight hours of insurance . . . an entire day of endorsements, deductions, premiums, coverages, declarations, claims, and endless phone calls.

It is a simple fact, she thought wearily, that I cannot stand much more of this. I will give my father until the end of the year, then he can come in and do something about running this place or he can sell; and that's whether I win or lose. Either way.

With that thought to comfort her, Carly walked to the private office overlooking the street, passing desks heaped with papers. File cabinets stacked with boxes lined both walls, and a huge iron safe stood sentinel beside her office door, its rusted wheels nested in little troughs of compressed flooring, the safe a testament to the honest construction of another time.

"Carly, you need to get yourself a helper. Someone to get you organized, keep track of meetings and speeches and things."

Carly shrugged and smiled at her sister. Except for Shellie's plumpness, the family resemblance was striking. "Like a girl friday? A boy friday? A campaign manager?" she asked.

Her sister nodded. "You'll make a good mayor, and it's time we had decent representation. This town is fast going down the drain."

"And you think I'll stop it?" Carly raised her eyebrows.

"Well, not stop it, maybe, but slow it down. This building and Pop's business are almost the only things left alive on Main Street. You've seen how everything else has moved to the malls or over near the university. And look at those trailers and buses parked back of town with no sewer system, all hooked to one water line, garbage piling up all over the place." Shellie lit a cigarette, took a furious puff and exhaled through her nose. "Half a dozen children at least are milling around there all day when they should be in school."

"Why haven't you complained to the police or the school board? That's what they're for, Shellie, to enforce laws already on the books."

"Ah, don't put me on. You know how many times I've called City Hall." Shellie grinned. "What it is, honey, is I'd like to be related to the town's leading citizen. You can fix tickets for me and get me out of jury duty, see to it that my taxes are lowered . . ."

"Now the truth comes out."

Shellie laughed. "Pop will be so happy. He always said you'd make a great politician."

"Well, we may have a chance to find out how great I am." Carly took a light jacket from the coat rack. "You're so organized, tell me where I'm going to find someone to help me run a political campaign."

Shellie opened the door and the two women walked to the elevator through the now quiet, empty office; the high ceilings caused their footsteps to echo like tiny hammer blows.

Carly held Shellie's arm. "Actually," she continued, "I knew I'd need help with the details but I didn't want to ask anyone here. These people are already carrying an extra load, what with Pop out for so long. I don't want to add to their troubles." Carly pulled the starter rope and the elevator began to grind its way to the first floor. "Can't you help me, Shellie?"

"I would do it, yes. But I can't. It'll probably take a lot of time and you know I don't have much of that. Buzz and the kids want me home when they're home."

Carly nodded, awed by her sister's ability to calmly balance the demands of a home, husband and three children. "Then help me find someone?"

"Sure." Shellie lifted the elevator's slatted gate, ducking under before the gate had reached the top of the opening. "Do you want to hire a man or a woman?"

"Either, I don't really care." They had reached the front door. Carly paused, her hand on the knob. "Shellie, I've decided something else, too. It's this place . . . the insurance business. Either Pop comes back to run it or we hire somebody to take over or we sell. But I can't do it anymore."

Shellie's jaw dropped. "Carly, why? What's wrong? You're doing a great job . . . we thought you were happy."

"I'm not. I've had insurance up to here." Carly gestured over her head. "It simply isn't my thing. I didn't mind at first because somebody had to do it. But I've had enough. I want out."

"Does Pop know how you feel?"

"No, I haven't said anything." Carly gave a quick little laugh and shook her head. "I told him I'd help temporarily, until he got well, but in his book that means forever. You know how he is. I wouldn't mind hanging in if I thought he'd be able to come back sometime soon." She sighed. "But it doesn't look that way, does it?"

"Does this have anything to do with running for mayor? Have we talked you into something else you don't want to do?"

Carly laughed. "Heavens, no! I've decided this is the best idea since the wheel. I'm excited about it. And I can't see that selling real estate precludes my being mayor. Roger Welles runs a law office in town, one in Bogalusa and one in Baton Rouge, and nobody thinks anything of his being the mayor, too. So why can't I be mayor and sell houses at the same time?"

Carly locked the door and the women crossed the street to Shellie's car. From behind the wheel, Shellie looked up at Carly, her face anxious. "Big sister, I'll help you all I can, you know that, don't you?" Not waiting for Carly to answer, she added, "And I feel so guilty for not realizing how we've imposed . . ."

"Hush," Carly interrupted. "I did what I wanted to do. Nobody forced me into anything. Now go home to your children."

Shellie nodded, but made no move to leave. "Pop called me this morning."

"I thought so. He told you about last night, didn't he? And you stewed all day until you couldn't stand it. You had to come see for yourself, didn't you."

"Well, I care about you. We all do. And I think you need more therapy. Those dreams have gone on too long, Carly."

"Let me be the judge of that, will you? Everybody has bad dreams once in a while. I think I'm entitled to mine . . . so bug off." Carly grinned to show that the words weren't spoken in anger. But as she watched Shellie drive away, the dream flashed in her mind. It was like watching a horror movie over and over, and her eyes grew wet with tears. It was all she could do to walk back across the empty street.

* * * * *

72

Ancient cypress tower over smaller trees growing in snarled clumps on the river's curve. Sunlight, filtering through the ragged growth, creates long shadows on a boat tied to a stump. The boat's occupants, a man and a boy, intently eye two red and white bobbers floating on the surface. From the shore Carly warns, "Time to go home. It's getting late and I've finished grading papers." She kneels to collect picnic things, aware that the quiet has been broken by the distant whine of an outboard. The sound becomes louder. Looking up, she watches a boat round the curve, its two motors roaring. Fearing that its wake will swamp the smaller craft, she shouts, "Hang on, he's going too fast." The driver, steering wide because of his speed, plows through the small boat and the two people in it. "No," Carly chokes. "Please, God. No!" The sudden cessation of sound is deafening. Carly, unable to move, watches a small bobber begin to drift in the current, its line trailing in the dark water . . .

Carly chose a Friday to interview the four people who had applied for the job. She told her father at breakfast, "I'll have the weekend to make a decision."

"Not too many wanting a temporary job, is that it?"

"No. The ones I'll see today know the job is part-time and not permanent. It's just that I don't know, myself, what's required." She shrugged and added, "Except for some as yet unspecified running around."

"Maybe I could do a bit of that for you, honey."

"Of course you could, but I don't want to impose. You do enough for me already." She pushed back her chair. "Thanks for breakfast. I'll call if I'm going to be late." Bending, she kissed her father's forehead.

"I didn't have any problem at all picking the campaign worker I wanted," Carly told her father that evening at supper. "I had given up hope of finding someone I could bear to be close to for the next couple of months. Until she walked in. Her name is LauraLee. LauraLee McCumber."

"A she, you said? What's she like?"

"Physically?" Carly paused to think. "Tall, I guess. At least taller than I am. Dark hair. Wavy. Blue eyes." Carly grinned. "You'd like her, Pop. She's slender, has a nice smile, great figure. Only I think she's too young for you."

"Does she know how to type?" Carl asked. "And how young is too young?"

Carly was in high spirits. "She doesn't need to type. Her father is a mayor and she helped with his campaign and is very knowledgeable about strategies and advertising and things that probably wouldn't have occurred to me." Carly paused, remembering LauraLee's enthusiasm. "Somehow we started talking about planning a campaign, and we talked so long she had to leave for her evening job before I thought to ask things like address and social security number." Carly drummed her fingers on the table. "It was really a matter of personality as well as qualifications. I liked LauraLee. We seemed to . . ."

Carly searched for a word. "We seemed to hit it off right away. Anyway, she's probably twenty-two or twenty-three, a graduate student at the university, so I'm sure she can type." Carly's smile told Carl her opinion of his concern about typing.

"If she's in school . . ."

"She's waiting out this semester. Budget cuts meant three of the graduate assistants weren't rehired, and LauraLee was one. She's working this semester so she can pay her way next term, in case the money's not there again. I think she's probably very poor."

"So are you paying her enough?"

"Actually, no." Carly paused. "Right now she's filling in at the university bookstore during the day and working at night in the diner out at the by-pass. Can you imagine how awful that must be?"

Carl shrugged, and Carly remembered that he felt that hard work built character.

"If she works for me full time, I can easily pay her more than she probably makes now at both jobs. Remember, I told you I intended to wait before I jumped into campaigning? Well, now I think I should get started." Carly was pleased with the thought.

After dinner, she kicked off her shoes, curled her legs under her, and began adding notes to a scratch pad.

"Planning your campaign?" Carl asked.

She looked up. "Not exactly. Just outlining a few thoughts. LauraLee talked about applying for grants to improve city services, balancing budgets, and inviting new business to locate in town. I'd thought it was just a matter of getting my name on the ballot, and then Shellie and her people would do whatever it took to get me elected. To me, the office seemed mostly titular, something anybody could handle with one hand. After all, there's no salary to speak of."

"But there's more to it than signing proclamations and cutting ribbons, Carly. That's why I didn't run when the Rotarians brought it up years ago. Too much politicking for a man with two little girls and a business to run."

"That's what LauraLee said, Pop. There's more to it than meets the eye, even in a small town like this. She said most of the voters don't know or care what goes on, but I needed to get my campaign organized anyway."

"Honey, you're beginning to sound like a politician."

"Am I?" Carly looked pleased. "I think I'll call LauraLee. There's really no need for me to wait. She can give notice this weekend."

Carl looked at his watch. "Won't she be at work now?"

"I don't know. Maybe. I'll try her house first and if she's not there, I'll call the diner." Carly took the scratch pad to the hall, saying over her shoulder, "At least I did get her phone number."

"I'm not sure what I want you to do first," Carly explained, smiling warmly, pleased that LauraLee had been early and that quitting both jobs had not caused a problem. But, now that she was here, how to fill the rest of the day? The women in the insurance office were always behind with their work, but LauraLee had not been hired to work in the insurance office. Carly was glad that she had made an outline to help get started.

Carly looked at her notes. "Is it possible for you to get a copy of the city budget from City Hall? And if we get federal grant money, I'd like to know what for and how much."

LauraLee was nodding. She had produced a pencil and pad and was writing as Carly spoke.

"Salaries," LauraLee said. "Let's also look into salaries for city employees. We talked about that Friday, didn't we?"

She looked up, and Carly was struck again by the deep blue of her eyes. She had remembered those clear, dark depths over the weekend. The clean line of LauraLee's shining hair was as she remembered it, too . . . A ponytail held in place by a ribbon tied in a simple bow. There was little artifice in LauraLee's appearance.

"Yes," Carly answered. "Salaries." Her thoughts turned to her own short hair and the silver starting to cover her temples. "You're looking very distinguished," Shellie had insisted. Carly saw that it only made her look old. Old and tired, her mirror told her. Why should I care, she thought, what difference can it possibly make?

LauraLee waited, but when nothing else was forthcoming, she offered tentatively, "Didn't you want me to fill out an application?"

Carly pushed back from the desk, nodding. "Of course, we'll get into that and we'll talk about rearranging some of this furniture so you'll have a place to work."

Carly watched through the door as LauraLee

walked down the center aisle, past the women busy with adding machines and computers. Each of them looked up and spoke as LauraLee passed; curiosity about the new employee would give them something to work over for days.

"Now," Carly said half aloud, "if I can find enough to keep her busy for a few days I'll have time to plan a campaign."

Keeping LauraLee occupied did not prove to be a problem. She spent hours at City Hall.

"It's probably a good idea to check out what went on in the last few elections, too," she told Carly. "See if any campaign promises were made, and if made, were they kept." She glanced at her notes. "Find out what the voters wanted. See what issues were important, and who said what and why. The weekly paper and the *Winston Daily Star* will have files I can check."

Nodding, Carly said, "Take as much time as you need."

By the end of the week, LauraLee had almost covered every page of her notebook with titled, itemized notations.

Carly leafed through the binder. "Did you have something in mind," she finally asked, "or is this simply basic research? What I mean is, what are you looking for?"

"Something to give us a focus when we start planning our strategy. There's always a rumor about bureaucratic corruption, and it would be careless of us to assume that every person working for the city is scrupulously honest, wouldn't it?"

Carly smiled agreement, not at all displeased with the plural pronouns.

"Ha!" LauraLee snorted, "I've seen enough to convince me that avarice is a basic political move, Mrs. Harrell. Greed, pure and simple. You won't believe what goes on."

Carly felt that she would, indeed, believe what went on. "When do you intend to share these revelations?"

"When you're ready." A new notebook was balanced on LauraLee's knees, a sharpened pencil stuck through the spiral binding, and LauraLee's small purse was propped against the chair leg. Her afternoon snack, a bright red apple, was balanced on her purse.

Carly suddenly realized that LauraLee was sitting on the only other chair in the office. "You need a desk, LauraLee. I think the attic is full of furniture so we'll take a look up there right now."

Together, they climbed the narrow attic stairs, wrestled open the door and peeked into a vast, black cavern, the only light admitted by the open door. The air was musty and dead.

"We need a flashlight." LauraLee sniffed. "Or a miner's lamp."

"I think we should give up this enterprise," Carly said sensibly. "Let's buy the desk."

"Wait," LauraLee whispered. "I see all kinds of interesting things . . . and some of them seem to be alive." She reached back. "Here, take my hand, we're in this together, you know."

Carly began laughing. They were inching their way along a cat-walk, narrow planks laid over the joists, and Carly knew that LauraLee couldn't see anything, either. "If I buy a new desk, can we get out of here? I think I'm claustrophobic." When LauraLee didn't answer, Carly said, "Also a chair with rollers and a cushion? I promise."

"Put it in writing?" LauraLee hissed over her shoulder.

Carly began giggling. "This is ridiculous but, yes, I'll stamp it in stone." She felt LauraLee turn so that they were facing, almost touching.

"I think we should stop meeting like this," LauraLee said in a deep whisper. "A cat couldn't find her kittens in here."

"What do you want to know?" The small restaurant had cleared of customers; they were alone in the booth section.

"The usual." LauraLee was very serious. "Why you're running, your qualifications, personal things . . ." She waited, pencil poised over her notebook.

"I hope you're ready for this," Carly said. She began ticking off points on her fingers. "I am a lifelong resident of Clearwater. I am a widow. I taught chemistry in the high school for eleven years. I now live with my invalid father, but before I started helping with his insurance business, I sold real estate."

When nothing else was forthcoming, LauraLee looked up. "That's it? That's all?"

"That's who I am and what I do." Carly managed to look offended. "What did you expect? Another Eleanor Roosevelt? Margaret Thatcher, perhaps?"

LauraLee's smile faded. She shook her head in disbelief and began writing in the notebook.

Carly watched in silence as long as she could. "LauraLee, what are you writing?"

For a long moment LauraLee didn't move. Then she looked up, her face calm, her glance innocent. "This is going to the local papers on Monday." She began reading, "Carly Harrell announces her candidacy for the office of Mayor of Clearwater, Louisiana. Her qualifications are nobody's business and her private life is not open to public scrutiny."

LauraLee's smile was positively evil. "That part will be free, because it's news," she said brightly. "They'll even print your picture. After this, however, we'll also buy space." She closed the notebook, slapping the pages together. "How do you feel about a full page photo? Just your picture and, in huge black letters, vote for Carly Harrell."

LauraLee was enjoying herself. She leaned forward. "We won't know your poll number for a while, but we can add it to the page when we do. Also, we need to contact all the civic clubs to get you on their calendar." Opening the notebook, she began writing as she spoke, "Item number one. Organize rallies, picnics, parades . . ."

Carly held up her hand. "Stop, I give up!"

"I thought you'd see it my way." LauraLee pointed her pencil at Carly, emphasizing each point with a little flick. "Soon you're going to be a public figure, so if you've ever robbed a bank, been a serial killer, had kinky sex with a room full of people, you'd better let me know so we can invent some lies to cover up."

Carly started to protest but LauraLee, her voice ominously soft, said, "You see, I'm serious about your campaign, but sometimes I'm not altogether sure you are."

"I am," Carly protested. "Yes, I am." And then, to her own astonishment, she blurted, "I've been more alive these past few days than any time in the last six years. I enjoy working with you, LauraLee. It's meant more than I can say."

LauraLee was suddenly very still. Slowly, she lowered the pencil. In the sudden quiet, they stared at each other. Then, her embarrassment growing, Carly fumbled for her purse and said, "It's getting late and Pop might worry. We'd better go."

"Sure. Remember your promise, though. You owe your campaign person answers to all questions asked, right?"

Relieved that an awkward moment had passed, Carly answered brightly, "Anything and everything, I promise."

"Shellie," Carly said, "Pop's not getting better. Doc called me yesterday. He said we'd better start thinking about bypass surgery." Visibly distressed, she added, "I don't know what to do."

"Why didn't you tell me Doc called?"

"I tried. I called from the office several times. I didn't want to use the phone in the house last night." Wordless, they stared at each other.

Carly said bluntly, "I have to file qualifying

papers in a couple of weeks. Perhaps I shouldn't."
She hesitated, wanting to be honest about her
feelings but not entirely sure what they were. "It's
just that planning a campaign, working with
LauraLee, has given me . . . an interest, a goal."
She looked into her sister's eyes, gray like her own,
and said quietly, "I haven't had nightmares since we
started, not one. I feel different, Shellie. As if I'd
been empty and now I'm not."

Carly bent to kiss her sister's cheek. "Have to
go."

"Wait, that's not all. We have to talk."

"Not now. I have to crank up that damn office."

"Let Sue do it." Shellie dismissed the insurance
office with a wave of her hand. "This is a family
problem and you don't have to take it all on your
shoulders." She poked Carly's shoulder for emphasis.
"You may be the big sister but I don't intend for
you to sacrifice any more of your life than you
already have." Before Carly could protest, Shellie
added tartly, "You have absolutely no social life, you
never go anyplace. What we'll do is dump the
business on Sue. Let her run the office, you run the
town, and I'll manage Pop." Shellie beamed, pleased
to have arrived at three such simple, yet workable,
solutions.

"Believe me," Carly said, "you won't have time to
care for an invalid. What about Buzz and the
children?"

"They'll make out okay. I know Miss Allie won't
spare Cora for the whole day, but we'll find someone
else to stay with him while you're busy doing official
things."

When Carly didn't respond, she added, "Come on

now. Don't start looking for objections. It's really time I did my share."

LauraLee, a constant whirlwind of activity, seemed to have every minute planned. Carly asked her, "Are you going to be in the office after lunch? My sister wants to meet you."

"Sure. I'm finished with City Hall and the newspapers. All I need now is your life story, if you please. You did promise, remember?"

"Yes, I did, didn't I?" Carly made a face.

"You gonna renege?"

"Of course not. I always keep a promise. Except when I don't." It was so easy to tease LauraLee, to laugh with her over pure silliness. Even when seriousness was called for, there was laughter lurking beneath the surface. She punched an intercom button. "Sue, take my calls, will you."

LauraLee rolled her chair across the bare floor, placing it so that she was facing Carly across the corner of the desk, the ever-present notebook open, a sharpened pencil in her hand. "I'm ready when you are."

"LauraLee, how much do we actually have to say?"

"The truth is, I'm not sure. But I do need more than you've already told me. My father's every move was in some paper or other. They'd do a kind of family story on all of us for the Sunday issues. So, if you have any secrets, you'd better count on somebody digging them up for publication." LauraLee stared out the window, a faint frown creasing her forehead. "My father's secret didn't stay secret long. I think it almost cost him an election."

"What was that?"

"I'm a lesbian," LauraLee said simply. "And in our God-fearing town that was worse than being a devil worshipper."

It seemed many minutes before Carly could speak. "Why didn't you tell me this before?"

"Why? Does it make a difference?" LauraLee closed the notebook. "Do you want me to leave?"

"No. No, of course not. But I would appreciate it if you'd close the door." She waited until LauraLee was seated again, needing those few moments to compose her thoughts. "May I ask you some personal questions?" At LauraLee's nod she continued, "Does your family support you financially?"

"Heavens, no! I'm persona non grata to my family and most of my home town. They couldn't wait to get rid of me once they found out. And that was my own dumb fault. I became involved with somebody who wasn't as interested as I thought."

"How long ago was this?"

"Five years. I finished my degree on my own, then I was accepted here in graduate school, but I worked for a year and a half to build up cash. I'm doing okay." LauraLee paused, waiting for a response. When Carly did not speak, she added, "I wasn't trying to hide my sexual orientation. I just don't think it should matter." Now her look was anxious. "It won't, will it?"

"I've already said it didn't. And it doesn't." Carly wanted to make sure that point got across, so she added for emphasis, "You can shout it from the rooftop for all I care."

LauraLee's smile was back. "Do we have to keep saying 'it?' Being a lesbian means I'm woman-oriented. I love women, but in other respects I'm like most females of our species."

"Do you have a . . . a roommate?" Carly didn't know what word to use.

"You mean do I have a lover? No. I've been alone for . . ." Smiling, she searched her memory. "For two years. My job, and keeping a four-point grade average in school, was more than Carol wanted to handle, so she split." LauraLee laughed. "It took me six months to catch up on the sleep I'd lost."

Carly did not want to dwell on the possible reason for that much sleep deprivation. She said, "I think you're a remarkable young woman." She faltered, went on, "I admire your courage." This was not what she wanted to say.

"Now that I'm out, so to speak, it's your turn. Let's talk about you." LauraLee's pencil was poised.

"Of course." Carly's tone was strained. She found, to her utter dismay, that she did, indeed, want to dwell on the thought of LauraLee and Carol engaged in the process of losing sleep.

It was almost two o'clock, but the campaign format over which they had labored all day still had gaps.

"These civic organizations only meet once a month, and they each have a program committee that schedules speakers way in advance." LauraLee swiveled her chair so that she could look down onto the street. "Doesn't your father belong to some of them? Couldn't we use him to get you on the agendas?"

Carly rubbed the back of her neck. "I'll ask him tonight." She stretched her arms to relieve tension. "Let's eat, LauraLee, I'm starving."

"Me, too." LauraLee turned to Carly. "Are your shoulders stiff?" she asked. "I'll give you a rub."

After a moment's pause, Carly pillowed her head on her arms. "Too much bending over," she said into the blotter. "I need a higher chair or a lower desk."

LauraLee's fingers moved over Carly's upper back and neck. "Can't you relax? Feels like I'm kneading a board. Are you . . ." LauraLee hesitated. "Are you afraid of my touching you? What I am doesn't rub off, you know." She said softly, "I wasn't making a pass."

Carly sat up. "I know that." Impulsively, she took LauraLee's hand. "Perhaps I am frightened. Just a little. Understand that I don't know any lesbians, so I need a little time to divest myself of . . . of the stereotypical pictures I'm carrying around." She tightened her fingers, felt LauraLee respond. "We're friends?"

LauraLee nodded. "Friends."

"Thank goodness. Now let's go eat some of that execrable cafeteria food."

"Seems like most of the women in town want to be involved, Carly. Contributions are up, and we have more volunteers than we can use. Your first mail-outs introduced real issues, honey, things voters have been bitching about for years. I'm impressed, I had no idea you were that politically aware." Shellie raised her hand. "No, don't interrupt, just listen. We plan to have an official send-off to launch your campaign, and we're inviting the whole town."

Carly looked horrified. LauraLee grinned.

"This will be a fund-raiser, a barbecue, a chance for you to do a little public speaking, and for the town to get to know you. We'll have balloons, the high school band, a clown for the children, paper hats with your name on them, flags all over the place."

In a tiny voice Carly muttered, "It sounds like a circus."

Feigning exasperation, Shellie said, "It *is* a circus. I thought you knew politics."

"Carly doesn't know anything about the American political arena. She's learning fast, though." LauraLee leaned forward. "Don't let this get out, but she's honest. She thinks everybody else is, too."

"I am not that naive," Carly protested. "I just didn't think it would all be so . . . so blatant."

Shellie looked at LauraLee. They both shrugged. "What can we do, LauraLee, to convince my sister that she has to win a *race?* Why," she asked Carly, "do you think they call it *running* for office?"

Carly simply shook her head.

"I gotta go. You keep her on track, LauraLee." Shellie ground her cigarette into the ash tray, lit another. "Don't forget, y'all, family dinner tomorrow night at Pop's." She nodded at LauraLee, her smile genuine. "I'm glad I finally got to meet you."

"Thanks, me too."

Carly watched Shellie exit the office, trailing a cloud of smoke. Carly tugged both windows as high as they would go. "Shellie's a whole smoke-filled room all by herself."

"Is your father going to do the cooking tomorrow?" LauraLee asked.

"No. Cora comes in four days a week. She's going to fix something extra tomorrow because of you."

"Me?"

"Uh huh. Pop thinks you're one part responsible for my . . ." Carly laughed. "My increased interest in life. Pop says . . ." Her voice trailed off, then picked up again. "I didn't mean that the way it sounded," she explained uneasily.

"Sounded okay to me. I understood what you meant."

Carly turned her chair to face the large, screened windows. Some of the buildings across the street were boarded, but a few with glass allowed a shallow glimpse into darkened space. LauraLee, too, stared at the empty store fronts.

"Shellie means well," Carly said quietly, "and she does have my best interests at heart." She leaned back, her fingers tightly clasped. "Remember I told you there was an accident?" LauraLee nodded. "Well, that was over six years ago. My husband and child were killed. I couldn't seem to stop grieving, the way normal people should. I began to re-live the accident in my dreams, in such increasingly horrible detail that I began weekly therapy with a group of people who had similar problems. It seemed to work for a while. Then it didn't."

Carly glanced briefly at LauraLee who was leaning forward, her concern evident. "I simply lost interest in everything. I quit teaching. I had Pop sell my house, I moved into a tiny apartment." She looked down at her hands. "I was so low I wouldn't have noticed a troop of baboons camped in my living room."

Carly crossed her legs, flicked absently at a speck on her skirt. "Shellie and Pop talked me into selling real estate from Pop's office downstairs. I liked selling. It was the busy kind of thing I needed, so I took the broker's exam. The dream . . . well, it stopped." She ran fingers through her short brown curls. "Pop had his heart attack, I moved in with him, took over management of both offices, stopped therapy. It's been almost two years." She looked at LauraLee. "A few months ago the dreams started again." Carly took off her glasses, and rubbed her eyes. "I think I'd begun to feel trapped, at a dead end . . ."

LauraLee waited. Finally, she urged, "And then?"

Carly smiled. "Well, now the dreams have stopped, and I'm sleeping like a baby. Also, I'm eating like a horse, and Cora says you're the one to thank. So she's going to thank you tomorrow with a super meal."

"Uh huh. I'm glad somebody appreciates me. I deserve every good thing I can get."

Carly was staring, as if seeing in LauraLee something she'd missed before. "Yes," she said, "I think so, too."

Cora had set a small table in the dining room for the three children, just like the adults' table except in miniature. The children, perhaps awed by the formality, behaved like the angels Shellie claimed them to be.

LauraLee waited in the living room with Pop and Buzz, while Shellie and Carly set out Cora's feast. They talked football, and basketball, and argued amicably over the Saints' not-quite winning season.

Later, when she could not stuff another delectable bite into her mouth, LauraLee waved her napkin. "I give up," she groaned.

"Honey," Pop said to LauraLee, "If you were a mite older I'd marry you just to keep you in the family."

Amid the general laughter, LauraLee looked across the table at Carly. Only you and I know how funny that really is, her look said.

Over coffee, Shellie described the plans for introducing Carly to the voters. "We're going to get the vote, that's for sure. Roger Welles doesn't have a chance against all the backing you have, Carly. I would say, conservatively, that you're a shoo-in."

"I hope so. How could I lose with all the good help I'm getting?" She smiled at LauraLee, who smiled back.

"Do you know how many speeches you've scheduled?" Pop asked.

LauraLee answered, ticking off on her fingers, "All the civic organizations in Clearwater, and all but the VFW in Winston, and they have to call me back about a date. We have two TV appearances in New Orleans, one in Baton Rouge. That's for starters."

"LauraLee, you've done a great job. What would Carly have done without you?"

What, indeed, thought Carly, would I do without her.

Strong hands cup Carly's shoulders from behind. LauraLee is whispering, a low, soft murmur that Carly cannot quite understand. LauraLee's touch is sensual, her fingers begin moving slowly, caressingly. "What are you saying?" Carly asks repeatedly, "What are you saying?" But LauraLee does not answer . . .

LauraLee was bent over the metal table, making dark squiggles on butcher paper with a felt tip pen. In the center of the paper, she had outlined what looked like an egg in its moment of hatching, and the wiggly lines under the cracked egg could have represented anything.

"Hi." She looked at Carly and grinned. "I'm trying out some spacing for a poster." With a flourish, she held the paper up in front of her. "What do you think?"

"I'm not sure." Carly barely refrained from laughing aloud. "It's so awful, I can't tell what it is." She assumed what she hoped was a thoughtful expression, and asked, "Do you want a serious evaluation, or just a few rude comments out of the hat, so to speak?"

LauraLee hung her head. "I'm crushed. You, of all people, should recognize the importance of my artistic efforts." With a snort she plopped into one of the folding chairs, the paper draped over her knees and touching the floor.

The sight of LauraLee's dark head bent in mock despair, the smile she was working to conceal, the lift of her breasts under the thin work shirt, her slender fingers with their square-cut nails . . . all of these suddenly seemed so precious to Carly that she felt her heart race. How good it would be to hold her, she thought, to feel that warmth and softness. Carly's eyes stung; the memory of physical tenderness seemed lost in time.

Needing to touch, she placed a hand on LauraLee's shoulder, saying gently, "Perhaps you should expend your efforts in some area other than fundamental design, my dear. If not, we may be elected dog catcher by mistake."

LauraLee swiveled slowly in her chair until her thigh pressed Carly's leg. Swallowing audibly, she looked up. "I have to go to the printer now for prices, then I'll call New Orleans and Baton Rouge. See what they'll charge for the same amount of work." She took in a deep breath, let it out slowly, then began rolling the paper up in her lap, her thigh warm and firm against Carly, her hands unsteady.

Carly did not speak, but neither did she move. So LauraLee said, "Anything else you want me to do?" And, after more silence, "I'll do whatever you want."

Carly said, "I know," then lifted her hand and moved away. It took a moment of fumbling for her to turn her chair so that she could sit in it. She pretended great interest in the contents of a file, not watching as LauraLee stuffed papers into a folder. Nor did she look up as LauraLee left. She stood at the window, watching as LauraLee crossed the empty street, then drove her sputtering car out of sight. She was still there, arms crossed, staring at nothing, when Sue entered, a sheaf of papers in her hand.

"Carly . . ." Sue said hesitantly. "Kenny and I have talked it over and if you want me to run the office, both of them, I'd like to give it a try."

"Sue, that's wonderful! You can start right now." Carly brightened. "That changes a few things. You'll need this office, so I'll rent an empty storefront for my campaign headquarters. I'll call Shellie and give her your good news, then I'll wait for LauraLee . . ."

After two hours of walking, and sorting keys, and climbing over shelves and counters, Carly decided that the lower floor of the building three doors from the Whitt Building was as good as they'd ever find.

"The front space is open, huge, and the walls are all one color. The carpet is clean, the bathroom's in one piece, there's a large private office and extra parking in back. What more could we ask?"

"Ummm." LauraLee frowned. "For a start, we can ask for a couple of dozen folding chairs, enough tables to line the side walls, a desk for you, lights, phones . . ."

"There's a rental place in Winston with everything we'll need. Call them while I get in touch with the owner and arrange for a short-term lease. You can attend to the utilities, too."

LauraLee was writing in her note pad. "Okay. We also need . . ." Carly's hand on her arm stopped her. Surprised, LauraLee looked up.

"You *were* making a pass, as you call it, weren't you?" Carly's words were not accusatory, her voice was gentle.

LauraLee did not pretend innocence. "Yes."

"Why?"

Face flaming, LauraLee shrugged. "Because I feel that way about you."

"Have I given you reason?"

"No. Yes! I mean . . . I don't know. I guess I thought so." LauraLee looked at the floor.

"Look at me, LauraLee. Don't hang your head." Carly's words came in a rush. "I do feel something for you, but it's not . . . not what you may want me to feel. Damn it, LauraLee, stop imagining what isn't there."

LauraLee blinked furiously, tried to smile. "I really should keep my thigh to myself."

Carly hooted. "If that's the worst thing that ever happens to me I'll consider myself fortunate. Now, are you listening to me?" She waited for LauraLee's nod. "I was upset this morning, and confused, but if you hadn't made such a point about being a lesbian, I probably wouldn't have noticed your . . . your thigh. LauraLee, to be honest, I am aware of you in a way that's different from any other person I've known." She paused as LauraLee's eyes widened. "Wait, you have to understand. This feeling doesn't mean I want to play knees with you."

LauraLee raised an eyebrow and asked guilelessly, "Then what would you like to play with me?"

Carly, shaking her head in mock amazement, said, "You're incorrigible. I can't imagine why I was upset over your foolishness. Would you believe I was going to spend the day away from the office, so I wouldn't have to face you."

Carly handed the briefcase to LauraLee. "I can't believe I was upset over some silliness that wasn't worth the effort I gave it. I'm certainly glad I realized it in time." She did not say in time for what. Instead, she handed LauraLee a ring of keys. "Here, take these back to the office, then meet me at my car."

LauraLee touched her forehead in salute. "I'm yours to command."

By ten o'clock the sun had evaporated the light fog that settled over City Park during the night, and volunteers were darting like spiders, stringing colored banners, nailing signs, setting out rows of wooden chairs. Four men in chef hats worked over two huge, metal barbecue pits, fanning charcoal and sending puffs of grey smoke into the cloudless sky.

Shellie, coordinator in charge, and taking her office seriously, was waving a clipboard, her oldest child clinging to her skirt. She shouted to a man pushing a dolly loaded with folding tables, "Have you checked to make sure the band will be here at eleven?"

"I checked, Shellie," he shouted back. "They'll be here."

"What about the loud-speakers? They're supposed to be set up already."

The man shook his head. "Not my department."

Shellie checked her clipboard. "Has anybody seen Bruce?" she yelled desperately. No one had.

By eleven-fifteen, a breeze from west of town was stirring the bright triangles of color strung from the band shell to tall wooden posts around the perimeter of the small park. The plastic flapped and crackled over the busy human sounds below. The band, scheduled to begin playing at eleven-fifteen, was nowhere near ready; the players were still unloading their instruments from the school bus.

"One, two, three, four. Counting, one, two, three, four. Can you hear me back there?"

"If he says that one more time I'm going up on that stage and kill him." Shellie was about at the end of her tether. She scanned the crowd, then stood. "They're coming now."

Pop, standing tall and handsome, held Carly's arm. They could move only a foot or so at a time because so many friends were crowding around. Shellie had to wipe her eyes, the sight was making her cry.

Once Pop was seated on the front row between Allie and Doc, Carly made her way to the stage. A few scattered cheers went up as Carly climbed the stairs, then someone began clapping, the cadence was picked up by most of the people milling around. "We want Carly, we want Carly," they yelled. Carly looked slightly startled, but she grinned at the crowd before taking her place on one of the chairs in the row behind the red, white and blue-draped dais.

As president of the Women's League, Shellie was seated next to Carly. Leaning so that she could be heard over the noise, Shellie handed Carly a straw hat and a typewritten page. "I tried to get this revised program to you last night, but you know how it is. We've changed the order somewhat, but you're still last."

Carly looked askance at the hat, then settled it gingerly on her head. "Shellie, this place is decorated like a used car lot. Did you have to?"

"Of course we did! Politics, my girl, politics. We're out to win!"

There were four speakers scheduled before Carly. "We told them to be brief," Shellie whispered, "but nobody checked to see if they knew what that meant."

Carly scanned the crowd, then turned to Shellie, "Have you seen LauraLee?"

"No. And I'm surprised. I thought she'd be here early."

"So did I. She was supposed to."

The band played "God Bless America," the crowd finally settled, and the speeches began.

Each speaker extolled Carly's virtues in much the same words, each spoke of Clearwater's history in glowing terms. In Carly's name, each mentioned progress, better management, opportunity, confidence, hope, and promise for the future. One even mentioned that the town's name should be changed from Clearwater to Dirtywater because the small river, for which the town had been named, had narrowed and flowed sewage from upstream for the last twenty-five years. This last drew cheers, laughter and boos, in almost equal proportion.

During all of this, Carly watched for LauraLee. She began to worry, trying not to imagine all of the things that could have happened. She was so distressed that she almost missed her introduction as the first woman to become mayor since the town's founding one hundred and seventy-three years ago. Shellie had to poke her to get her attention.

Carly's carefully thought-out speech, for which she did not use notes, was based on the theme of meeting the challenge. She did not specify which challenge.

She spoke of working together to effect changes in the mayor's office. She did not elaborate on the kind of changes the office needed.

She pointed to the audience and told them that, together, they could make a difference. Then, briefly, she outlined the differences that she envisioned, and gave details on how and why the townspeople should make the attempt.

She promised her undivided attention to public services, public facilities, public protection. She smiled, she was modest, aggressive, knowledgeable, compassionate, committed, and the crowd loved her. It should have been a perfect moment.

She had planned, as her closing words, to describe the value to Clearwater of having a concerned mayor. Then she saw LauraLee standing behind the last row of seats. LauraLee with a young blonde woman. They were not listening to Carly. They were looking at each other, and they were absorbed in their own conversation.

Carly swallowed hard, forced a smile, held up

both arms and said the only thing that came to mind, "Enough talk. Time for food!"

The crowd roared, the band began playing an approximation of "Happy Days Are Here Again," and Carly tried to make her way down the steps and through the throng, to LauraLee. But too many hands were outstretched, too many well-wishers wanted a word, so her forward progress was slow. Pop was beaming and wanted to congratulate her, to introduce her anew to some of his business friends, to hold her arm. She could not break away, nor did she see LauraLee again.

She nibbled at the obligatory barbecued chicken, choked down a swallow of coleslaw, sipped cola, and smiled, smiled, smiled. The rally had been a triumph, by small-town standards, and Carly should have been elated.

Finally at home, she dialed LauraLee's number. There was no answer.

Sunday morning, the phone rang before Carly and Pop had finished their first cup of coffee. Carly knew it was LauraLee. But it was Shellie, wanting to know how Pop had weathered the excitement. On the heels of that, Cora called to say she was sending a platter of sliced roast beef, vine-ripened tomatoes, a container of gravy, a loaf of french bread, and potato salad for their lunch. Supper was to be at Allie and Doc's, if Pop felt up to it, and if they weren't obligated elsewhere. Carly said she'd let Cora know after Pop's afternoon nap.

Carly had planned to spend part of Sunday

outlining what she wanted to say during the TV interview in New Orleans on Wednesday afternoon. This was not to be a political speech but an expression of Carly's views as a newcomer to politics, on the subject of political integrity. Carly did not plan to repeat the time-worn platitudes she'd spoken on Saturday. No, this was an opportunity for her to give an honest evaluation, and she had found, somewhat to her own surprise, that she had very definite opinions on the subject. Her ideas required refining, however, if they were to be fitted into an hour long show, much of which would be taken up by commercials.

She sat at her desk, flipped open a lined pad, and sharpened several pencils. She moved the phone closer. It rang. Not LauraLee.

An hour later the pad was still blank, the pencils sharp, and she had answered the phone four more times.

Cora's hot roast beef and gravy made deliciously sloppy po-boys. Pop ate, Carly wasn't hungry.

Pop, still excited over the New Orleans and Baton Rouge Saturday evening TV coverage of the rally — albeit brief — wanted to go to Doc's for supper so he could talk about it. Carly wanted to stay home in case LauraLee called. She was too proud to try calling LauraLee again, too hurt and too angry.

Throughout the day, she had tried to analyze her feelings but there seemed to be no rhyme nor reason to them. Could she, for instance, be jealous? Jealous? How silly, she thought. Of course not. Anyway, jealous of whom? The blonde woman? Was the blonde at the rally the Carol who had split from

LauraLee two years ago? Were they now together in bed, doing whatever it was those women did? Carly's mind went blank at this point, and she ground her teeth. Why this agonizing over a person whom she'd put out of her life once the elections were over, win or lose?

Before they left the house that evening, Carly was tempted to forward calls to Doc's. But she didn't. I hope you call, she thought. I hope you call and call and I'm not here.

The wheels of Carly's car screeched as she snapped around a corner. I am not dependant on LauraLee for anything other than the help she can give me on this campaign, Carly thought, and I did not need her there on Saturday. Everything went quite well without her. She muttered, "I will be forty-three years old next May, and I am perfectly able to handle, on my own, whatever needs handling." She pulled to the curb, taking no notice of the papers and files that flew into disarray when she slammed on the brakes.

Sue was in the private office, working at Carly's old desk. Carly saw that LauraLee's desk was gone, as were the folding chairs, table, and LauraLee's desk chair. She was stunned for a moment, then she tapped her forehead with a finger. "Can you believe I forgot this is your office now? I'm going to make a great mayor, that's for sure." She turned to go, then stopped. "Has LauraLee been in?"

"She was here before any of us. I think she's over in the new building. Something about furniture coming from Winston." Sue stood. "Saturday was great, Carly. You're a wonderful speaker."

Pleased, Carly nodded. "Hang on to that, Sue. Doc told us Sunday night that Roger is going to fight to keep the office. This is the first time he's had active competition, so he's planning something or other to get the vote. Count on it, the good-ole-boys will be out back-slapping any day now."

"Won't do them any good, Carly. The voters are solid behind you. Why, half the town was there Saturday, and Kenny said it was the biggest turnout for a political rally he's ever seen."

"I think most of the turnout was for the food, but maybe we gained a few votes. I'm gonna hang in."

The storefront was locked. Carly peered through a front window at chairs and tables and boxes, apparently dumped haphazardly in the middle of the room. She banged impatiently on the glass.

"If you'll hold these, I'll unlock the door. You forget your key?"

Carly whirled to face LauraLee. "What key?" she snapped.

"The one I gave you Friday." LauraLee was holding a sack and two plastic cups. "Take these and I'll unlock the door," she said patiently.

Scowling, because this was not the way she had

planned to greet LauraLee, Carly watched without speaking as LauraLee unlocked and opened one of the glass doors.

"After you, ma'am," LauraLee said, standing aside.

The room, which had looked so big last week, now seemed small and definitely cramped. Carly put the bag and cups on the seat of a wooden chair, then turned to LauraLee, saying the thing she had promised herself not to say. "What happened to you Saturday?"

LauraLee reached for the bag, looking down so that Carly could not see her eyes. "I was there for your speech, then I had to leave." She held open the bag. "Take a donut, please. The jelly ones are on top, plain on the bottom. And take a coffee. Either one, they're both the same."

"You didn't answer me." Carly, furious, wanted to shake her.

"Yes, I did." LauraLee was very busy taking the plastic lid from one of the cups. She took a bite of jelly donut. "I was there in time to hear you, then I had to go." She licked at jelly oozing from the pastry. "A friend came to town. We had a lot to talk about so we went to my room to talk." In apparent fascination, LauraLee stared at the donut, then took a sip of the steaming coffee.

"Was this the person you told me about?" Carly heard the words come out of her mouth, the question she'd vowed not to ask. Even to her own ears, she sounded like a police officer interrogating a prisoner.

"My ex, you mean? Yeah, that's who it was." LauraLee nodded, hungrily taking another bite. "She wants to come back. Seems it wasn't so bad with me, after all."

"And?" Carly's mouth went dry. For a terrible instant, LauraLee's face flickered out of focus. Like a tape spinning out of control, Carly's mind began to whirl through all of the stated, sensible reasons she did not need LauraLee, did not want LauraLee. Then the reel clicked into normal speed, and she realized, she knew, that she did want LauraLee, did need LauraLee, in whatever form that need would take. "And?" she asked again, in a whisper.

"And, what?" LauraLee gulped coffee, looking everywhere but at Carly.

"My God, you're exasperating! You know damn well what! Is she or isn't she staying?" Right or wrong, Carly had no intention of sharing LauraLee with a scrawny, frizzled blonde.

"I thought you'd know the answer to that without asking." LauraLee searched the bag, gingerly extracted a plain donut, then, staring into the greasy bag, and apparently deeply concerned with the contents, she said, "These are both for you. Better eat, they get stale fast."

Carly realized that she had known the answer without asking. "Put down the bag, LauraLee." Obediently, LauraLee placed the bag on the chair. "Now, look at me."

LauraLee looked directly at Carly for the first time. Carly saw anxiety and fear. Lightly she touched LauraLee's chin. "You were worried about what I might do, weren't you?"

105

LauraLee nodded. Carly smiled grimly. "Then we both had a perfectly wonderful weekend, didn't we?"

"Ha, speak for yourself."

"I think I just did."

Together, with the help of Shellie, various volunteers, and two handy-boys from the high school, they cleaned and vacuumed, set up tables and chairs, put LauraLee's small desk outside the door to the room which was to be Carly's office, and had a large desk delivered for Carly. Carly objected, but Shellie hung streamers anyway, and one of the ladies painted out the bottom half of the plate glass windows.

"I have a sign painter coming on Wednesday to do the lettering for your windows. The grand opening's Friday night, this place is going to be jumping." Shellie was overflowing. "Wait and see."

Carly shrugged, saying dryly, "You certainly have an ability to get people stirred up, Shell. I simply cannot wait." Carly tried looking to LauraLee for help, but Shellie and LauraLee were seeing eye-to-eye as far as decorating the headquarters was concerned. Especially did they see alike in the matter of food.

Near noon, the refreshment-committee ladies brought a cold lunch, moved tables to the center of the room, and set up places for anyone who dropped by. The noise level around noon was unbelievable, but the picnic-like atmosphere was so successful that they decided to bring lunch for the rest of the week.

"You have to work on your TV interview," Shellie

said, "so you do that in your office. We'll finish collating and addressing these mail-outs. Honestly, Carly, we can handle everything out here without your constant supervision."

Carly reluctantly agreed. It was not easy to sit alone in a bare-walled room, listening to the activity taking place on the other side of the wall, so she took her pad and pencils and sat at LauraLee's desk. That way, she could work and still be a part of the group.

The TV interview was to take place in New Orleans at four-thirty. Carly and LauraLee were at the network station in New Orleans by three.

"If you behave, maybe later I'll treat you to dinner at a fancy restaurant." Carly had said this as they crossed the causeway.

"Phooey! What's a fancy restaurant compared to the food we've had these last couple of days?" They were both stuffed from lunch, but Shellie had packed emergency rations anyway. The plastic bag, filled with sandwiches, salad and cake, rested in a cooler on the back seat.

Carly shrugged. "Suit yourself. You'd probably disgrace me, anyway."

"Keep it up," LauraLee warned.

They had ridden in silence most of the way, each happy with her own thoughts, and with the presence of the other. They had not spoken again about Saturday's rally, or about Carol.

"Shouldn't you go over what you're going to say?" LauraLee prompted.

"I don't have to. I know that I know what I know."

"Okay, Gertrude. But what if he throws you a curve? The guy who does the interviews isn't all that hot on women in politics."

"Then I'll light a fire under him." Carly assumed her most superior expression and said, "There's very little he can ask that I can't answer, my girl. Have no fear, I am his equal and then some." Except, Carly thought, if he asks about my feelings for you. I can't even answer myself on that one.

In the interview, Carly was serious, non-threatening, yet honest and direct in her answers, and the show host responded. Carly listened in amusement to his lengthy, convoluted questions, which she then answered in clear, simple terms.

"You were wonderful," LauraLee told her afterward. "You were perfect."

The show over, back in the car, Carly said, "It's too early to eat, isn't it? Let's do some shopping."

"Fine by me."

They walked the length of the mall, Carly, in high spirits, holding LauraLee's arm.

Carly gave in first. "My feet have collapsed. If I don't sit soon I'll need crutches.

"Maybe we could eat now?"

"Eat." Carly appeared to debate the point.

"Ummm. Eat what's in the car, or go someplace where we can sit in comfort, and be waited on? And be served something hot? There are plenty of places near here."

"That sounds fine."

There was a light fog, which made everything seem fuzzy, but the restaurant's tall neon sign shone like a beacon. They were offered a table, but Carly asked to sit in a booth. The booths were very private. "So I can kick off my shoes," Carly explained to LauraLee in a whisper.

The meal took a couple of hours. They ate, they talked, they had extra cups of coffee, a little wine. They lingered.

By nine o'clock the fog had closed in, shrouding the lakefront area. The Pontchartrain causeway had been closed an hour before, except for emergency vehicles which would be convoyed across by state police. The causeway would open for convoys, in both directions, when the fog began to lift in the morning, nothing else until then. Not unusual for the time of year.

Carly said, "We'll either stay in a motel, or go Airline Highway to Baton Rouge, then back-track. But that would take hours and who's to say the fog hasn't closed those roads too."

"I vote for the motel," LauraLee said.

Carly was feeding quarters into the vending machine. Her words came in a rush: "You can't pick your toothbrush color, but you can select the kind of toothpaste you want. They even have tiny bottles of mouthwash. Do you have a preference?" She pushed coins into the slot and jerked a knob. She knew she was talking too much.

Clutching a yellow toothbrush and a small bottle of green mouthwash, LauraLee followed Carly back to their room. It was the usual . . . two double beds, a round table with a hanging lamp, two chairs, a low chest of drawers.

"I have to call Pop and Shellie before it gets any later, to let them know what's happened. Why don't you shower first?"

LauraLee nodded.

Carly placed the call to Pop first, then called Shellie to ask her to check on Pop first thing in the morning.

Then Carly sat, her heart pounding furiously, listening to the shower noises. She knew what was going to happen next. They were going to lie together on one of the beds. There, Carly would take LauraLee in her arms, would feel the soft warmth of LauraLee's strong body. This was a fact, incontrovertible. This was what Carly's senses told her. This was why she wanted LauraLee. The wanting had nothing to do with the campaign, not with posters, or TV interviews, not with speeches or rallies or votes. Finally honest with herself, she admitted that she was sexually excited by LauraLee, and had been from the moment they met.

The shower sounds stopped. Almost breathless, Carly closed her eyes, picturing LauraLee naked and wet. Then LauraLee was standing in front of her, wrapped in a towel, little tendrils of damp hair on her forehead. "Were you falling asleep sitting up?"

Carly swallowed. "My turn?" she asked brightly.

LauraLee, her eyes so deep they seemed black, nodded and moved aside so Carly could stand.

Carly took longer than usual in the shower. Her hands were trembling, she kept dropping the tiny bar of soap. Then she bound the towel tightly around her and opened the door. LauraLee was waiting, and Carly walked into her arms.

They kissed for what seemed hours. Pressed together, they breathed into each other, tongues touching. Their movements caused the towels to loosen and slip to the floor. Carly moaned aloud when she felt the pressure of LauraLee's soft naked body.

Slowly, LauraLee moved her hands down Carly's back, reaching as far as she could. She cupped Carly's buttocks, pulling Carly's body hard against her own. Carly moaned again when she felt LauraLee tighten against her.

LauraLee's breathing was ragged. She led the few steps to the bed, then lowered Carly to it, her knee between Carly's legs. She leaned on both arms, and looked down into Carly's face. Carly, her eyes glazed, pulled LauraLee down, and they kissed again, Carly's hands stroking LauraLee's shoulders and arms. Then LauraLee's soft mouth claimed Carly's breast, and Carly's body arched as she clamped her legs tight around LauraLee's thigh.

"You're ready . . . you're ready . . ." LauraLee breathed.

Carly's heat and wetness spread as Carly moved her hips, rubbing flesh on flesh.

"You're so ready . . . ready . . ." The words were a chant, hardly heard over the harshness of their breathing. LauraLee began moving her thigh to match Carly's rhythm. "Ready . . ." she said hoarsely, raising her head until their lips touched again. Then she shifted to Carly's side, and placed her hand in the softness between Carly's legs.

"Ready . . . ready . . ." she intoned, her fingers stroking, seeking, finding.

Carly was helpless. With what strength she had left, she gripped the spread on either side and dug her heels hard into the mattress, thrusting against the movement of LauraLee's fingers. She opened her legs wider. "Please. Oh, please."

"Yes," LauraLee promised. "Yes."

"I love you."

Carly looked up into eyes that were a deeper blue than the deepest sea. She could happily drown in their beauty. She smiled.

"I love you," LauraLee said again, her breath touching Carly's cheek.

"Ummm," Carly said. She put her hands on either side of LauraLee's face and gently drew her down until their lips met. "Ummm. Soft, so soft."

LauraLee kissed Carly's eyelids, her nose, her chin, her mouth again. She lay propped on an elbow, half covering Carly's body, a hand free to explore the smoothness of Carly's breasts. With her index finger, she traced circles around a hardened nipple, then leaned and took the raised flesh into her mouth. "You taste better than candy," she murmured.

"I thought I was floating, higher and higher," Carly said softly, stroking the dark head that lay on her breast. "And you were my only contact with the world."

In a pleased voice, LauraLee asked, "When I was inside you, you mean?"

"Yes. I couldn't feel anything but you. Your touch, and what you were doing." Carly sighed. "I had no idea."

"You liked?" LauraLee wanted Carly to say it.

"I had never imagined . . ." Carly paused. "Yes, I liked," she said simply. "Like" was not adequately descriptive, but Carly felt LauraLee understood.

Carly had wanted to touch her lips to LauraLee's; she had fantasized gentle embraces and soft touches, but her mind had raised nebulous, wavering boundaries beyond which she had not dreamed. The image had not included the sureness of LauraLee's touch as she guided Carly to the bed, or the reality of LauraLee's smooth nakedness.

It had definitely not included the sight of LauraLee's bright head now moving over Carly's thigh, or the feel of LauraLee's tongue inching its way through Carly's thick crush of pubic hair.

"Oh, no." Jerked out of post-coital lethargy, Carly fumbled for purchase on LauraLee's arms. "No, LauraLee. Wait." Not *that*, her mind whirled, not *that*.

She caught at LauraLee's hair. "Wait," she pleaded, "wait."

LauraLee took a deep breath and said softly, "No."

Carly felt LauraLee's tongue again, just above the hairline, burrowing downward, daintily touching with a gentle side-to-side motion. LauraLee's hand slipped between Carly's thighs, separating them. Then, her mouth still pressing, she settled her body into the space.

"Raise your knees." It was a command.

With a low moan, Carly grasped at LauraLee's hair, tightened her thighs. "Oh, please," she gasped, "please, I don't think . . ."

LauraLee's voice was muffled, rough. "Don't think. Just feel."

Carly felt pressure as LauraLee's elbows pushed outward, a soft pressure, but Carly did not have the strength to resist. With a sob, she raised her knees, felt LauraLee's hands press against her inner thighs, pressing until her legs opened their widest. In the next instant, she felt LauraLee's fingers gently separating her inner lips, brushing aside hair, and then the velvet of LauraLee's tongue.

Carly's eyes squeezed shut; pleasure began spiraling through her with a liquid motion, one wave following so close on the other as LauraLee's fingers sought, found, and entered the moist opening. Carly heard someone groaning, as if in great pain, but the waves were moving through her with such force that she could not focus on any need but her own.

Carly felt heat and wetness and an exquisite pressure, but nothing had prepared her for the thrust of passion that pierced her body when LauraLee's mouth enclosed her clitoris. LauraLee's tongue encircled, LauraLee's fingers pressed . . . and Carly cried out again and again as her body arched in orgasm.

* * * * *

Carly spoke softly into LauraLee's ear. "I want to do that to you."

They were lying under the spread, LauraLee's leg and arm resting across Carly's body, her hand cupping Carly's breast.

"Well, I'm glad you're back with me."

Carly smiled. "Yes, I am definitely with you."

"Let me ask you something? It's none of my business, and you don't have to answer if you don't want to."

"Is it that serious?"

LauraLee sighed. "Not serious, curious. Was tonight your first orgasm?"

"Why are you asking?"

"Because you seemed so surprised. As if you didn't know what was happening."

Carly took in a deep breath. She spoke slowly. "Well, yes. At least the first recognizable one."

"What does that mean, recognizable? You were married, had a child . . ." LauraLee stopped abruptly. "I didn't mean to say that."

"It's all right, I don't mind." Carly stared at the ceiling for a moment, then raised herself on an elbow and looked into LauraLee's eyes. "Larry and I had sex as often as any other couple, I guess. He always initiated it, and I was willing; not enthusiastic, after a while, but willing, because I loved him and that was what you did when —"

LauraLee interrupted. "Please, you don't have to say anything. I really didn't mean to pry."

"I know you didn't, but I'd like to tell you."

Carly lay back and LauraLee snuggled tighter against her. "I think," Carly began, "if I'd complained it might have been different, but I didn't know there was more. And neither did he, obviously. Having sex was pleasurable, especially the closeness, the sharing, and Larry was satisfied so I didn't think about it too much. Having a child, finally, proved that I must have had sex." Carly sniffed and tightened her arms, "I know it sounds crazy but that's how it was."

LauraLee could not see Carly's gentle smile. "There was never, ever, anything like this . . . this wildness with you."

"You liked what I did?" LauraLee had to keep asking.

"Oh, yes."

"You want to do that to me?"

Softly, "Yes."

Carly's fingers lightly stroked LauraLee's lips. Her breath quickened as LauraLee drew the fingers into her warm mouth and began sucking. She felt the tingling tightness begin again between her legs.

LauraLee released the fingers and whispered, "I certainly hope so because I'm about to explode!"

LauraLee's legs moved apart. "Touch me. Put your hand here."

LauraLee guided Carly's hand across crisp hair, then down between smooth thighs to warmth, to softness, to wetness. LauraLee's voice was hoarse as she said, "Feel how much I want you."

Carly made love to LauraLee. She stroked the flesh that moved to meet her fingers. She pressed her lips against the fullness of LauraLee's breasts, tasted LauraLee's sweetness, felt LauraLee's heart thudding wildly as their bodies strained together, her own heart pounding loud in her ears.

The room's TV flashed a background of alternating light and dark on the walls, the audio covering the joyous sounds of their lovemaking.

Deepening with each minute, the fog enclosed the motel in a cloud of swirling dampness. Traffic stopped. The nearest sound was the sizzling of the motel's neon sign, flashing unseen in the mist.

"You awake?"

"I think so," Carly whispered softly.

"I have to move my arm, but I didn't want to wake you." LauraLee nuzzled Carly's neck, her breath warm on the soft place beneath Carly's ear.

Carly kissed what she could reach of LauraLee's hair. "Is your arm asleep?"

"No. It's dead." LauraLee, groaning, slipped her arm from beneath Carly's neck. "Wonder what time it is?"

"Not morning yet. But close, I think."

LauraLee was busy wrapping herself around Carly, tightening as close as the stripes on a peppermint stick. "Plenty of time," she whispered. "Plenty of time."

"Are we going to make love?"

"Yes."

Carly, knowing the form their lovemaking would take, said, "Let me shower first."

"That's not necessary."

"I know it isn't, but I'd like to anyway. Please?"

LauraLee sighed. "Only if you hurry."

Carly untangled herself from LauraLee and the covers. She sat on the edge of the bed, and looked at the little she could see of a naked LauraLee. A LauraLee only partly covered by the heaped bed clothing.

"If you keep looking at me like that . . ." LauraLee threatened.

"I'm going." Carly stood, evading the hands that reached to pull her back to the bed.

"Think I'll bathe with you," LauraLee announced, pulling back the covers.

They soaped each other. They kissed, hands moving freely over slippery flesh, fingers exploring.

As LauraLee knelt, Carly held her shoulders. "Please, let's go back to bed." She leaned to turn off the water, LauraLee's arms snug around her.

They were both dripping wet. "Lie on the edge of the bed," LauraLee said. She grabbed a pillow, dropped it to the floor, then knelt on it, and lifted Carly's legs, one to each shoulder.

As LauraLee's mouth came toward her, the memory of LauraLee's lovemaking became crystal bright. It created a feeling so sharp that Carly's breath caught. She widened her legs in anticipation, her thighs tensed, and she pushed forward to meet the thrust of LauraLee's tongue.

The fog was still heavy when the second convoy of cars headed north across the lake. Carly drove at the required speed of fifty miles an hour, trying to keep the taillights of the car ahead in sight, but not too close in case there was need for a sudden stop. The fog was even deeper on the lake; it was like driving through heavy, grey clouds. Her headlights, reflecting back, bathed the interior of the car in an eerie glare. They had not spoken since getting in line.

"What have we done?" The words were whispered but LauraLee heard.

Slowly shaking her head, and not taking her eyes from the glow of the taillights ahead, LauraLee said, "You mean what are we going to do now, don't you?"

For half a mile Carly didn't answer. Finally she nodded. "Yes, that's what I meant." She glanced at LauraLee. "I know what we've done," she said, "but I don't know what we do now."

"I'm not sure I do, either."

They rode for several miles, the only sound that of the engine. Finally LauraLee said, "You live with your father, and I have only a bedroom with kitchen privileges."

They considered that for another mile.

"I wasn't only thinking about where we'll go to make love. I think we can work that out somehow." Carly sighed. "It's . . ." She sighed again. Nothing in her experience had prepared her for the dilemma which she now faced.

LauraLee moved closer. She touched Carly's cheek. "Do we have to work it out this minute?" She moved even closer, and Carly reached for her hand, holding it tightly.

LauraLee pulled Carly's hand to her lips, kissing each finger. "Can't we stay like we were?" she temporized. "We have a lot of work to do on your campaign, and I think we should, maybe, get on with that, don't you?" She didn't wait for an answer. "What I want is to be with you every minute, and you know it. But I don't see how we can manage

119

that, so let's do what we can and . . . and wait and see. We don't have to decide this very minute, do we?"

"You're right, of course." Carly smiled in relief. "If we ever get off this bridge I'll take you home so you can bathe and change, and then we'll meet at the office just as if nothing happened."

LauraLee breathed a happy sigh. They rode another few miles without speaking, their hands clasped.

"Was it your intent to starve me to death, or do you expect us to eat the stuff on the back seat?" They could hear water sloshing in the cooler.

"Why, no," Carly said. "We're going to eat at the waffle place near the interstate." She looked at LauraLee. "I'm glad to see your appetite hasn't diminished overnight. I'd worry."

"Nothing about me has diminished overnight." LauraLee grinned. "In fact, I'm probably happier right now than I've ever been. In my whole life."

"Did I make you happy?" Carly's question was serious and the answer mattered very much. She wanted, more than anything, to know that their lovemaking had been perfect for LauraLee, too.

"Yes," LauraLee answered instantly. She tightened her fingers. "Remember that I love you."

The storefront was jammed, there wasn't an empty seat. "Brought here by the promise of food, no doubt," Carly whispered to Shellie.

"How can you say that? You were magnificent

yesterday. I'll let you know we had a crowd here watching you on TV, and that took place after we'd served the food. So there."

"Hi, soon-to-be-Mayor Harrell." It was LauraLee, beaming. "Hear you made a hit with the locals yesterday."

Carly turned, her throat suddenly dry. "So they tell me." She waited a moment, then added, "Think you can shop with me in Baton Rouge this evening? I need something special for tomorrow night."

"Okay by me." LauraLee grinned at Shellie, and said, "Now I'm going to dive into what's left of the food. I'm starving." LauraLee's heightened color delighted Carly. She knew what LauraLee was hungry for.

"She's a great kid," Shellie said to LauraLee's retreating back. "Buzz and Pop both fell for her."

"Good taste runs in the family," Carly said dryly.

The motel room had one double bed but, as Carly pointed out later, they only needed one bed. They were in each other's arms within seconds after the door was closed and locked. Another few seconds, and they were on the bed, still clothed, clinging, kissing.

"I thought we'd never get here." The motel was thirty miles from Clearwater. "I was about to attack you in the car." Then LauraLee was lying on top of Carly, holding Carly's head between her hands, moving her tongue in Carly's mouth.

It took but a moment for Carly to capture the

rhythm. She closed her lips around LauraLee's tongue, felt the beat of her heart thudding between her legs as their tongues danced together.

LauraLee was in no hurry. She continued the motion, her tongue sliding between soft lips, and into sweet moisture, lingering, withdrawing, pressing inward, sliding out . . . slowly, at first, then faster as Carly's breath caught with each thrust. Carly pressed upward, her hips straining against LauraLee's weight, her hands pulling LauraLee closer.

"I want to love you," LauraLee said, rolling to Carly's side. Refusing Carly's help, she opened the buttons of Carly's blouse, pulled slip and bra straps down, and kissed Carly's shoulder, the soft swell of Carly's breast.

"Let me undress."

"No, this way. I want to love you this way." LauraLee freed one nipple. She leaned to it, and took the hardened flesh into her mouth. She bit lightly; Carly jerked. She bit again. Carly's hands touched her head, urging more.

"Love me," Carly said.

LauraLee lifted Carly's skirt, pulled it out of the way, and touched the smooth flesh at the top of Carly's legs. Carly made little sounds, little movements, her breathing became rapid, irregular. LauraLee's fingers fumbled the elastic band of Carly's briefs aside, so that she could reach in, touch Carly's flesh, dip into Carly's moisture.

Carly groaned when LauraLee touched the smooth, erect knob that seemed to be floating in a pool of warm liquid. LauraLee stroked, her fingers circling, her movements only partly restricted by the silken fabric. Carly strained, lifted into her. LauraLee pressed her cheek against Carly's forehead.

Carly turned her head aside, freeing her face. Her mouth partly open, she began breathing in short, quick gasps, her hips raised, unmoving. LauraLee, one arm under Carly's shoulders, squeezed Carly to her in a fierce embrace, still guiding her fingers around and over the tiny protrusion. When she felt Carly stiffen, heard Carly's quick inhalation, she moved her fingers faster. Then Carly sighed and her body relaxed.

LauraLee waited until their breathing slowed, then withdrew her fingers. She straightened Carly's skirt. "I love you," she whispered.

Carly, her eyes not quite focused, stared up at LauraLee. In a very small voice she said, "I'm not sure I remember the sequence. Could we do that again?"

They left the room soon after ten o'clock. They had made love, rested, made love. Carly drove LauraLee home at a snail's pace, unable to bear the thought of parting.

"I want to spend a whole night with you," LauraLee said. "I want to wake up in the morning and feel you next to me."

"What about a whole weekend, would that suit you, greedy?"

"Maybe, maybe not."

"Tomorrow night is the party. We'll try to get away afterward."

* * * * *

By six-thirty there wasn't an empty chair. The room had been redecorated, and balloons floated everywhere. Two of the refreshment servers were busy icing down champagne, and other aides were setting out napkins and stacks of brightly-colored plastic plates.

The finger sandwiches were still covered, but people were sneaking handfuls, anyway. Huge inroads had also been made in the platters of cookies, brownies, rum balls, and pralines. Only the hot table, loaded with tiny meatballs and spicy sausage, remained untouched, and that was because serving utensils had not yet been set out, and there was no way to scoop the steaming morsels out of the thick gravy.

Shellie was furious. "If they don't stop gorging, there won't be anything left when the party begins."

Carly and Pop had gone by for LauraLee, so the three of them arrived a few minutes before seven, Pop between LauraLee and Carly, who was wearing a black crepe dress. People clapped, and a cheer went up. Pop turned to LauraLee. "I didn't know I was still so popular," he whispered.

Carly was eyeing the decorations. "Shellie," she hissed when her sister embraced her, "do you have an interest in a balloon factory?"

"No," Shellie hissed back. "But I do have an interest in getting you elected, my dear sister. Now smile, you're on camera."

Carly smiled. She shook hands, she kissed, she hugged, she spoke to everyone in the room.

124

Even from across the room, Carly felt LauraLee's gaze, and she knew exactly what LauraLee was thinking. LauraLee was looking at her watch every few minutes; Carly, also.

This was not a night for major speech-making. Carly introduced the special invited guests: a state senator, two Clearwater council members who were running for second terms and thought it wise to change to the winning side, and Judge Elmore Whitt, Carly's great uncle on her father's side. Each said a few words, then Carly thanked the crowd for coming, encouraged them to vote, thanked them again.

Shellie said to Pop, "That was the shortest political speech in the history of political speechmaking. She had a captive audience, why didn't she take advantage of it?"

"She probably won more votes by not talking. Give Carly credit, she knows what she's doing."

They had let Pop out in the driveway. "You have your keys?" Carly asked for the second time. She didn't want to drive away until she was sure Pop could get into the house. "We'll probably stop for coffee, I have a mental list that needs to get on paper before I lose it. You'll be all right if I'm not back for a while?"

"I'll be snoring like a baby in five minutes. Take your time."

* * * * *

"You're so beautiful . . . so beautiful . . ." LauraLee was sucking Carly's swollen nipple, her tongue circling the dark outline. "I wanted you so much tonight, I could hardly stand it."

Carly stroked the dark head hovering over her breast, smoothed her palms on LauraLee's strong shoulders. "I could tell," she whispered.

"How long can we stay?"

"How much time do you need?"

"A lifetime."

"Oh, my darling." Carly guided LauraLee's mouth to hers. Their kisses were soft, lingering, their lips separating for an instant, their breath mingling. Soon, LauraLee began an in-out motion, inserting and then withdrawing her tongue from Carly's mouth. Carly's breathing quickened, and her lips remained parted, inviting LauraLee's tongue to move deeper with each tiny thrust.

Passion built quickly. With a low moan, Carly shifted her hips and spread her knees apart. This was invitation enough for LauraLee. She cupped Carly's vulva, fingers quickly becoming lubricated as they moved within the velvet folds, finding and gently stimulating Carly's clitoris.

There was no question but that LauraLee would make love to Carly first. It had been this way since that fog-bound night in New Orleans. LauraLee initiated, Carly followed. Neither thought to question the fact that Carly was more quickly aroused, or that Carly reached orgasm with a minimum of foreplay. Making love to Carly heightened LauraLee's desire, often creating excitement that exploded with Carly's first, loving touch. They both liked it this way.

LauraLee knew that Carly was ready. She tightened her arm under Carly's shoulders, her fingers still moving, stroking, probing, teasing the smoothness of Carly's vaginal opening. Carly sobbed in anticipation. LauraLee pressed her lips to Carly's. Carly strained against her hand.

They parked in front of LauraLee's rooming house.

"Tomorrow's Saturday," LauraLee said. "How will I live without you?"

"You won't have to. We're going to the coast tomorrow morning and not coming back until Sunday night. I have it all figured out."

LauraLee's eyes widened. "How'd you do that?"

"Simple. We're supposed to be going to talk, informally, to a group of ladies who've invited us for the night. They're having a late dinner for us on Sunday, and we'll be back as soon as we can get away." Carly frowned. "I'm not really very good at lying, but I think my story sounds plausible, don't you?"

"You could fool me. But I'd believe anything you said, so I'm not a good test."

"I'll pick you up after breakfast . . . about nine o'clock." Carly reached for LauraLee's hand. "Be ready, because I have a surprise for you."

LauraLee looked down at their clasped fingers. "Carly, don't buy anything for me, please. I can't . . . I don't have enough money to get you anything. I'm kind of bothered already about you paying for the motels."

"Don't say that. I have more than enough." Carly's laugh was short. "The accident left me a very wealthy lady. Money simply poured it." She paused. "I haven't spent a dime of it, because I've had nothing to spend it on. But I'll hold off. I don't want to make you unhappy."

LauraLee, obviously trying for levity, said, "Now you know the reason I want you. I'm after your money, lady."

"Hush. It's my body you want, not my money."

LauraLee hung her head. "Would you believe I want you again, right now?"

"Yes," Carly kissed LauraLee's fingers, unmindful of the eyes that might be watching a parked car with two women in it. "Yes, I'd believe it."

The days flew faster than Carly could ever remember. She was challenging a "good-old-boy" system of government, and the voters in Clearwater's sister-city, Winston, were watching with interest.

Carly's campaign was also causing a stir in the entrenched political systems around the state. Carly often felt like a dervish, whirling between meetings, dancing a tightrope between the factions that sprang up as the campaign gathered both heat and speed.

"Pop, being mayor may not require a full-time person, but running for office is a twenty-four hour, seven-day job."

Carly wasn't really complaining, however, because the demands of her campaign also gave her opportunities to be alone with LauraLee.

They spent the night once in Baton Rouge, one wonderful weekend on the coast, and once more in the New Orleans motel of the fog. When it was possible, they managed a few evening hours in one of the motels on the northern outskirts of Winston and, once, an overnight stay in Plaquemine, where Carly was featured speaker on Public Ethics at the PCC annual awards banquet.

Carly hated sneaking and lying, especially lying to Pop. The lying and sneaking did cause an element of strain, but it was a tiny faultline. It did not cause a problem in their lovemaking, but often gave Carly pause.

"I'm really not cut out for this," Carly said to LauraLee one night in their motel room.

"What?" LauraLee turned on the light. "What are you saying?"

"I hate this sneaking around, LauraLee. I'm always on guard, always afraid I'll give us away by looking at you, or touching you. I hate having to invent excuses for us to be together, and I don't like feeling guilty all the time."

"Carly, please hush. We've been through this before."

Carly nodded. She touched LauraLee's breasts, cupping their fullness, teasing the pink nipples. Then, with a sigh, she pulled LauraLee down, whispering, "Yes. But we're a May-December romance, my love, and I can't find a happy ending . . ."

LauraLee was close to tears. "We're not, we're not! We're Carly and LauraLee, not May and December. Please don't look for an ending when we've hardly gotten started! Promise me, please, promise me." The tears began to stream, dripping on Carly's bosom.

"Do I mean that much to you?" But Carly knew the answer. It was the answer Carly would give if LauraLee asked the same question. As LauraLee nodded, Carly said, "Then I promise. With all my heart, I promise." And Carly always kept a promise.

LauraLee was beaming. "We're winning, Carly. You've really turned this place on its ear. I think this is the first election in Clearwater's recorded history that has a political battle with real issues." She turned to Shellie. "You know your sister is going after that illegal land fill in the swamp? Well, the only way to clean the river is by stopping the pollution from north of here. That means no more untreated sewage from upstream, no more run-off from the dairies or the gravel pits —"

"This will hit a few pockets," Carly interrupted, "but most sensible people should see the need."

"Don't let this out, but we've uncovered something really bad." LauraLee leaned forward. "The city got matching federal money to replace the pump on the town well, but most of it was spent on a gravel road from the highway out to Ed Lester's camp and Ed is Roger Welles' brother-in-law."

Shellie shook her head. "I hate to hear that."

Carly showed Shellie a computer printout. "This is for Pop. He and Cora take turns calling registered voters. Pop says they're exercising their rights as citizens. They're influencing the electorate."

"Pop also says you're out very late a lot of evenings but he's not worried. And when you have to go out of town, dear sister, we both think you *should* stay overnight to keep from driving after dark. It's dangerous for two women to be alone on these country roads at night."

Carly eased her tongue through LauraLee's crisp pubic hair, seeking, then finding moist, soft flesh. She felt the weight of LauraLee's legs on her shoulders, a weight that pressed downward as LauraLee raised her hips.

With her fingers, Carly searched for the smooth entrance, enjoying LauraLee's wetness, and the low moans that now urged speed.

LauraLee reached between her legs and grasped Carly's hair. "Don't wait . . . don't wait." She lifted her hips, "Please, Carly . . ."

LauraLee's legs contracted, making it hard for Carly to move but, by this time, movement wasn't absolutely necessary.

LauraLee groaned. "Carly," she breathed. "Carly."

"I won't see you for the whole weekend, do you realize that?" LauraLee said.

"You were invited."

LauraLee grunted. "I don't have the kind of clothes to meet a governor. I'd feel stupid among all those fancy-dressed people."

"I told you I'd buy whatever you wanted to wear."

"And I told you I didn't want you to buy clothes for me," LauraLee snapped. "You already pay for everything."

"Well, I'm the one with money," Carly answered sensibly. "If you had it, you'd buy what I needed, wouldn't you?" She offered what seemed to be a reasonable solution. "I'll just not go."

"Oh, come on! You have to go, we both know that. What it is, is that I feel you moving away from me." Tenderly she touched her lips to Carly's. "I am simply afraid to death of losing you. What will we do when you're mayor and I'm back in school? We'll never see each other anymore. Look how it is now . . . we have an hour together now and then." LauraLee groaned aloud. "Carly, I am so in love that I'm going crazy."

"I know, my darling, I know," Carly said softly. She thought of reminding LauraLee that they had promised not to speculate about a future together. "Damn it! I'm sick and tired of this." Her voice became steely. "I'm buying one of those new condos in Winston and you're going to move out of that stupid room . . . and you're not going to give me any crap about who's paying for what." Her hands jerked LauraLee's shoulders. "Do you hear what I'm saying?"

"Oh, no . . ." LauraLee began defiantly.

"I will not listen to your silly objections, LauraLee." Carly was shaking her for emphasis, none too gently. "I'm going to do what I'm going to do, and you're going to do what I tell you to do about this . . . understand?"

"I'm not —"

"Oh, yes, you are." Carly, excited by the beauty of her idea, pulled LauraLee to her.

Neither Carly nor LauraLee heard the crunch of gravel as the maroon car drove through the parking lot. They did not see the driver stop behind Carly's car to write something in a small notebook, then slowly drive on to the far end of the parking area and stop, lights out. Only the tiny, orange glow of a cigarette showed that the car was occupied.

Carly was working at her desk when Pop came down to breakfast. He bent to kiss the top of her head. "Hi, sweetheart. Y'all had a good night?"

"Sure did. We got a lot done." She held up some papers. "I'm not a pollster, Pop, but our figures put me so far in the lead that Roger won't stand a chance."

"He's called me twice in the last week or so, you know. We used to be pretty good friends."

"I know that, Pop, but he's on a lot of lists right now. Remember when the Mothers' Club wanted that downtown lot cleared to use as a playground? Well, Roger blocked it, and they've never forgiven him. He also sold the Little League park to that trailer dealership, remember?"

Carly shoved the papers into the desk drawer and stood. "How are you feeling?"

"Haven't felt this good in a long time. Cora and I

are going to begin walking again today. Doc says it'll be good for both of us."

"I'd like to stay in New Orleans tonight, Pop. There's a meeting this afternoon that I know will last forever, and I hate crossing the lake at night. Especially if there's fog." Especially if there's fog, Carly thought, remembering the first time she and LauraLee had made love. Since that wondrous night of discovery, fog had held a special place in Carly's heart.

"LauraLee's going to move from her rooming house, Pop. She's taking one of those condominiums in Winston, and we'll probably spend some time tomorrow looking for furniture. She doesn't own a thing, so we'll check out the warehouses on Tchoupitoulas, and Williams Boulevard. Maybe do a little scouting on Magazine Street, too."

Carly finished her coffee. "We'll try not to be too long at it, but it'll be late Saturday, I'm sure, before we're back. You'll remember to take your pills?"

"Of course, I'll be fine." Carl thought for a second. "Tell you what, honey. You look for something she'd really like to have and buy it as a housewarming gift from me." His smile was broad. "I really like that girl."

Wednesday, October 25

"And so, Bernadette, Friday morning was the last time I saw my father." Carly cleared her throat. "The last time before his stroke, that is. LauraLee and I drove to New Orleans that morning, shopped, arranged for delivery of the things we'd bought, then checked into a motel."

Even after all that she'd told me, Carly blushed like a school girl as she added, "We didn't leave the room until late Saturday afternoon."

I blinked, glad that I hadn't told her about Albert Junior. It was too obvious that there could be pictures. It seemed to me that Carly and LauraLee had been as discreet as a herd of elephants charging down Main Street.

"Bernadette, I need something to drink. Would you like another glass of beer?"

I heard amusement in her voice. Carly was out of the rocker and in the kitchen before I replied.

"No thanks, Carly, I have to go to the bus station for Vi." I leaned in the doorway, watching Carly put ice in a glass. She was probably waiting for some words of wisdom from me, so I said, "I don't know exactly how to help you, but give me a little time, will you? And for goodness sake, don't tell another soul what you've told me. Not Shellie, not Buzz, not LauraLee, understand?"

Carly nodded. "If you say not."

"I say not."

"What if . . . he calls?"

"Put him off. Say whatever you have to, but don't commit yourself to doing anything. No meeting, no money, understand?"

I left then, tired from sitting so long, heavy-hearted because I couldn't see any way to help her, and more than a little envious of LauraLee.

It stood to reason Albert Junior was the blackmailer, but the blackmailer could be someone else, someone who had the pictures that would kill Carly's reputation once and for all. Psychological suspense was part of a blackmailer's game. Was that why he hadn't called back? The more frightened Carly was, the more she'd pay, of course. Then again, he might not have called because he was already dead and laid to rest. Then too, who had killed Albert Junior? Someone in this town was a murderer, a murderer not likely to be caught.

I had gnawed my thumbnail to the quick by the time Vi's bus pulled into the lot. "I am certainly glad you're back," I said as I led her to the car.

On the way to Aunt Allie's, I stopped at the Cash-and-Dash market, parking as far from the pumps as I could. Telling Vi took an hour, but I wanted to be thorough. I didn't feel that I betrayed Carly's confidence; I needed Vi to help me think this through, and I knew that the weight of the pyramids couldn't squeeze a secret out of her.

"Oh, honey," she said when I finished. "Poor Carly is really in a mess, isn't she?"

I nodded. There was simply nothing I could say.

Vi said, "If Albert Junior had a partner, Bernie, perhaps that's who killed him."

I wrestled with that for a minute.

Vi shook her head slowly. "No, I just can't see a partner. What I know about Albert Junior tells me he wouldn't have shared this. He didn't need to. He knew Carly, knew enough about her to feel sure she wouldn't tell anyone. Telling would be admitting her relationship with LauraLee, and that's what she wanted to keep secret, isn't it?"

"Yeah. I can't fault them for falling in love, Vi, but they couldn't have played their love song any louder if they'd sent announcements. It was all out there for anyone with eyes."

This made Vi laugh aloud. "Like us?"

"Aw, we weren't running for public office, nobody was watching us."

"You keep believing that, my love. With an IQ

higher than the national debt, how can you be so unaware at times?"

This stung. There was truth in what Vi said, but when I seemed blank to her, it was because I had my mind focused on a problem, usually something to do with the lab. Something I couldn't share because she didn't have the technical background.

Like music. I loved to listen, but all I could say was that I liked this, didn't like that. I couldn't give a technical reason. Vi and Agnes could chatter music in in-depth detail for hours, leaving me in the cold. I didn't mind, I couldn't even hum the most simple tune.

Backing to the street, I said, "I'm never unaware. It may seem a trance-like state to you, Vi-vee-an, but I'm in there chugging away all the time."

"Well, chug us to Aunt Allie's, I have to go to the bathroom."

"Carly called," Cora said as we walked up the stairs. "She wants you to call her back."

I did, then told Vi that we were going to Carly's to meet LauraLee. "Supper, too."

"How nice. I wonder what she's like, this LauraLee?"

"Guess we'll find out soon enough." I, for one, couldn't wait to see the person who'd snared Carly after all her years of celibacy. What kind of person was this who had finally turned Carly on? Too bad it couldn't have been me those many years ago. But at that time I was hardly more than a child, unsure of my sexuality, and she was grown-up, married and years older. Now, the differences in age didn't seem to matter. Vi was Carly's age, or not far from it, and LauraLee was twenty years younger. Ah, me.

I gnawed my remaining thumbnail. I didn't really want Carly, I think it was the memory of wanting her that haunted me. I turned to look at Vi.

She was looking at me. "It bothers you, doesn't it?"

"What do you mean?"

"You know what I mean. You haven't gotten over wanting Carly. It's not something you're going to do anything about, but the feeling's there."

I tried for laughter. "The sound you just heard was the nail being hit square on the head." I won't lie to Vi. "I can't explain it. She told me about falling in love with LauraLee, and I felt jealous."

"No, darling, not jealous. When you become privy to the story of their growing physical passion, it turned you on. I know you."

I shrugged. "You think that's it?"

"I *know* that's it. If it wasn't broad daylight, and everybody still in the house, we'd head back to Aunt Allie's and I'd take my baby to bed." Vi lifted her eyebrows. "Want to rent a motel room?"

"Yes."

"Do we have time?"

"No. We're there." I pulled into Carly's driveway.

Carly met us at the door. "LauraLee is going to be a few minutes late. Her car fell apart so I lent her mine. She's at the garage now."

"Anything we can do?"

"Thank you, no. Usually I have Pop's car to fall back on, but it's at the station. The lights and the key were both turned on, so the battery was

139

completely drained. Pop doesn't drive much, and we don't know what he had in mind, or where he planned to go."

"Friday night, when he had the stroke, you mean?"

"Yes, and it's the strangest thing. He was in the car when Shellie found him, but we don't know if he was coming or going. Come, we'll wait in the den."

"I don't understand," I said when we were seated. I darted a glance at Vi.

"Well, Pop's car has mostly been in the garage since his heart attack, and I usually leave mine in the driveway because I'm too lazy to put it in the garage. So most nights there hasn't been any room for him to back his car out. But Friday night and Saturday the driveway was clear because I was away in New Orleans. Pop must have decided that he needed something, or had to go someplace, and we can't understand why he didn't call Shellie. He could have called Doc, too, or any of a dozen people. There was simply no reason for him to drive himself anyplace, especially at night."

"It must have been important to him, whatever the reason."

Carly nodded. "I imagine so. Poor darling, he was carrying a large sum of money, too. Wilbur Thornton had cashed a check for him Friday afternoon. We think he was going to make a cash contribution to my campaign."

"Shellie found him Saturday morning?"

"Yes, about seven-thirty. We have no way of knowing how long he'd been lying there. The car door was open and Shellie said he was half on the seat . . ." Carly's eyes filled.

"Why was Shellie here that early?" I didn't want to see Carly cry.

"She was going to fix breakfast because I was out of town, and Cora doesn't help out on weekends. Bless her heart, Cora's been our rock."

I began gnawing what was left of my nail. "Yeah," I said absently, "Aunt Allie would be lost without Cora." My mind was not on Cora.

I looked around the room. It was part of a huge house, reflecting an earlier time when craftsmanship was important. The ceilings were tall, the rooms spacious, and the polished floors gleamed. I knew Vi would be impressed. I wondered if Cora did all the housekeeping, too.

"Your house is the same as I remember, Carly. I don't think a thing's been changed."

"I don't think much has. Pop and I are really lost in this place, we only use half of the rooms, maybe fewer. My grandfather had it built to hold a large family, but it's hard to heat and harder to cool." Carly paused, cocking her head to one side. "I hear LauraLee, will you excuse me for a moment?"

Vi waited until Carly was out of the room, then turned to me. "What is it? You've thought of something?"

"You bet I have. I'll tell you later."

We waited a few minutes, neither of us speaking. Vi broke the silence. "I know what you're thinking. I just put it together."

"I'm going to call Donald again. Have to ask him to run through a few things for me, won't I?"

Vi nodded slowly. "You could be wrong, Bernie."

My answer was cut short as Carly entered the room, a tall, dark-haired young woman at her heels.

Carly reached back and their hands met. The young woman stepped forward to stand at Carly's side. "This is LauraLee McMurray, my assistant." Carly put her arm around LauraLee's waist, nodding toward me, then Vi. "This is Bernadette Hebert, and her lover, Vivian Barr."

We could tell that Carly had done some briefing because LauraLee didn't seem overly startled by the introduction. Her smile was tentative, but she nodded to us. "Hello, Doctor Hebert, Miss Barr," she said quietly.

Vi decided to end the awkwardness. She stood, extending her hand. "Call me Vi, everybody else does. While we're on names, Bernadette is known as Bernie now. Only Aunt Allie and Doc call her Bernadette any more."

"I'm really glad to meet you," LauraLee said. "We don't know any other . . . any other lesbians. Carly thinks we're the only two in the world." LauraLee seemed to be at ease now. Probably because the "L" word had been said, and not one person had fallen dead, or screamed, or fled from the room.

I got to my feet, grasped LauraLee's hand. "It's good to meet you, LauraLee. I hear you're the genius behind Carly's campaign."

LauraLee smiled and looked at Carly. "Is that what you're telling people?"

"Yes, because it's true. I wouldn't be at square one, but for you."

Their gaze met, seemed to lock, eliminating Vi and me from the room. I could feel the heat from where I stood.

We sat on the sun porch to eat Cora's dinner, balancing the plates on our knees. Very much at ease, I told Vi and LauraLee about my mishap spilling the beer. It was a comfortable evening, full of laughter. Carly did not seem to be under any strain at all, she was totally in control. She and LauraLee sat together on the couch, touching frequently. Before we left, we set a date for Carly and LauraLee to spend a weekend with us on the Gulf, depending on the condition of Carly's father, of course.

On the way to Aunt Allie's, Vi said, "You see that I trust you implicitly. Would I deliberately expose you to a weekend with Carly Harrell otherwise?" Vi was serious.

I grinned as widely as I could. "In the words of our famous governor, *you* are my sunshine, my *only* sunshine . . . and so forth." Then I asked, "You're kidding aren't you, Vi?"

Vi took her hand from the wheel and patted my thigh. "Of course I am."

I called Donald. We talked for a long time. I told him what Carly had told us, what I surmised.

"We're probably right," I said to Vi when I hung up. "Donald thinks so, too."

"Dear God, how awful. Are you going to tell Doc?"

I walked to the window, folded my arms, stared down at the street. I shook my head. "No." I continued staring. "Yes."

Vi didn't want to influence me either way, so she didn't speak. She knew I would do what I believed to be the right thing. But what was the right thing?

She sat very still, watching me become a silhouette against the fading light. "I want to help you, my darling," she finally said. "But you have to live with the consequences, so you must make the decision."

I turned. "I'm going to tell Doc."

"When?"

"I don't know. Now. No, tomorrow."

"I think he's going back to the clinic tomorrow. Cora said he has to catch up after cancelling so many appointments. I think getting back into his routine is probably the best thing he can do."

I stared at Vi. "He's here now, isn't he?"

Vi nodded.

"Come with me?"

We went into the small parlor, and Doc closed the door. He pulled a chair in front of the sofa and sat facing us. "You know something." He clasped the chair arms and leaned slightly forward. "Tell me."

I spoke slowly, but this was my way when I wanted to get everything in the right order, so that there could be no misunderstanding. "What I suspected has been confirmed by someone who, at my request, looked into Albert Junior's murder. We believe —"

Doc blurted, "Who did it, damn it! I don't want all that — just tell me who it was!"

"Don't yell at me!" I was up in a flash, glaring. I felt my face getting redder by the second.

Vi jumped to her feet and stood between us. She said over her shoulder, "Bernie, sit down!"

It was her school-marm voice. I sat.

"And you," she said to Doc, "you keep your mouth shut. If you want to learn what Bernie knows, then you sit and listen or we're both leaving — this instant, do you hear me?"

He heard. Reluctantly, he nodded. Vi looked at me. "Now, Bernadette, you may begin." Then she sat, and I could see that she was holding back laughter at our astonishment.

I took a deep breath, then told Doc about Donald, about the investigators who'd checked the owner of each license plate. That they'd found nothing to lead them to believe that any one of the suspects, nor their family members, had had anything to do with Albert Junior's death. "It was a blind alley, Doc." I didn't give him my list of names; there was no reason for him to know Carly's name was on the list.

My recital faltered. I looked helplessly at Vi. Vi smiled and nodded slightly, so I began. "We think Carl Whitt killed Albert Junior."

"What?" The word exploded from Doc's mouth, he jumped up. "You can't be serious!"

"I'm serious. He had a motive, Doc. He had opportunity."

"That's not a crime. You could say that about half the town."

Ignoring Doc's comment, I said, "If you'll listen, I'll tell you what we think happened."

Doc sank back in the chair, his expression one of disbelief.

"I'll keep it simple, and you can ask questions when I'm through, understand?"

After another swift glance at Vi, I began. "Albert Junior must have contacted Mr. Whitt, and threatened to expose something he thought Mr. Whitt would rather keep out of the public eye. Either Albert Junior actually knew something or he invented something, but only Mr. Whitt can tell us that.

"On Friday afternoon, Mr. Whitt withdrew ten thousand dollars from his bank, in small bills, on the pretext that he was making a cash donation to his daughter Carly Harrell's campaign. There was no reason to give Carly's campaign that much money in cash. He had already donated a large sum, by check. Anyway, Carly doesn't need the money. Her campaign fund is spilling over. The ten thousand was to pay blackmail to Albert Junior."

Doc grunted something, which I ignored.

"Mr. Whitt hasn't been driving since his heart attack, and this is on your advice, Doc. We believe that on Friday night he took his car out of the garage, and drove to the subdivision. There he met Albert Junior, killed him and drove home, only to have a stroke in the driveway of his home. Shellie found him Saturday morning, as you know." I paused for breath.

"Where's the shotgun? Where's Albert Junior's wallet? How do you know Carl went out Friday night? He may have gotten in the car minutes before Shellie found him Saturday morning. Bernadette, I think this is foolishness."

"No, Doc, it's what happened. Mr. Whitt probably threw the shotgun and the wallet into one of the streams under the highway, or into the swamp. He could easily have done this from his car, and we could look from now till doomsday and not find either one. When Shellie found him, the car battery was dead because the lights had been left on from the night before. Albert Junior was killed between twelve-thirty and one-thirty, or thereabouts, and the car lights would have drained the battery in six or seven hours."

Doc snorted. "This is crazy."

"Crazy, yes. But that's what took place."

We hashed out each point, one by one. Doc was finally convinced that I was describing what must have happened. He sat, hunched, his face pale. He said to me, "Carl won't recover, we don't know why he's still alive. My God, what will this do to Carly?"

"To Carly?" I felt my jaw drop. "Why should this do anything to Carly? She doesn't have to know. I don't see that anybody else has to know, either. What good would it do? Mr. Whitt is dying, so let it be, Doc. You've known Carl Whitt for forty years, let his good memory stand."

Doc thought about that for a long time. We waited. "You're right," Doc said. "Even if he did kill my son. What purpose would it serve? He wasn't the kind of man to take the law into his own hands." Doc shook his head sadly. "Carl must have been desperate to do what he did . . . desperate and driven. He wouldn't have done it without a damn good reason, and I guess Albert Junior must have given him one."

"I'm glad you see it that way," I said. "It wouldn't help a thing to let the truth get out of this room. It wouldn't bring Albert Junior back." I looked into Vi's affectionate gaze, her encouraging smile, and added, "I can't show you actual proof, I've no evidence that can be presented in court. At this moment it's supposition, but it fits, it all fits."

I was glad that it hadn't been necessary to tell
Doc that Carl Whitt's reason for the killing was as
big as a mountain. Carl was protecting his beloved
child who had already suffered the death of a
husband and child. Reason enough to kill . . . even
Doc would think this.

Doc said, "I'm not going to tell Allie, either.
Carl's death is going to be a blow, but if she had to
face this other . . . I don't think she could manage."
He sat in thought. Then he stood. "Thank you,
Bernadette. And you, Vi. Knowing . . . helps."

Thursday Morning, October 26

After we left a tearful Aunt Allie, we drove directly to Carly's storefront. "We're on our way to the coast, can you have coffee with us before we go?"

I think Carly could tell by my expression that I was the bringer of good news. It was a gorgeous morning, and I felt great. Fortunately LauraLee was out on an errand. We sat in the car, drinking from plastic cups. "Don't spill it, Bernie," Carly said. Vi snickered.

"Keep it up, y'all," I warned, not at all bothered. I was in good spirits, and feeling better than I had all week. We hadn't gone to a motel, but we had made love, slow and easy, last night, and again this morning. Vi certainly knew how to erase Carly from my thoughts. I felt like we were on our honeymoon, and I couldn't wait to get to the privacy of our camp on the Gulf.

"Carly," I began, "I told Vi your . . . about the blackmail and all. I really needed to get her impressions. Okay?"

"That's fine, Bernie," Carly said. "Now, what do you have to tell me?"

I turned so that I could face her. "Carly, what I'm going to tell you is in the strictest confidence." I paused for emphasis. "We think that Albert Junior was your blackmailer, and that he was killed by someone else he tried to blackmail. There's not enough evidence to bring the killer to trial, but he's not likely to kill again." Every word of this was as true as I knew it.

"What about pictures?" She wasn't ready to accept her good fortune. "Do you think this other person has . . ." She couldn't even say it.

I could say it. "You mean will he try to blackmail you with Albert Junior's pictures?"

"No, my dear," Vi interrupted. "There were no pictures, Albert Junior was lying." No reason to tell her that there may have been pictures, but, if so, they were resting at the bottom of the swamp, where her father had thrown them.

Carly looked to me for confirmation. I nodded. "No pictures, Carly. You don't have to worry. Get on with your life."

Carly's smile was something to remember. She reached across the seat to touch Vi, then me. "I can't believe it's over," she said. "But I've learned. Never again will I be afraid or ashamed of who or how I love."

We were on the road, heading east. "You know, Vi, I'd make a pretty good detective, don't you think?"

"You already do very well in the crime lab. Why not stick to what you know?"

"But I'm good at deductive reasoning. Didn't I solve a murder?"

"Keep your eyes on the road, please."

"Well, didn't I?"

"Of course you did, but you don't have time for another career, my dear."

"Seems to me I could find time."

Vi leaned and spoke softly. "I have things for you to do, my darling, that will take up whatever extra time you have."

Epilogue
November 25

"Go back in the woods and get all those rotten fence posts. We're going to burn them on this pile of leaves."

"It's gettin' late, Aunt Cora. Can't we do it tomorrow?"

"Do as I say, boy. Bring it all right here."

Cora watched as the pile of old wood grew until it was almost waist-high. "That's enough. Pour that kerosene all over it, then give me the matches. You go home now."

She waited until her nephew had rounded the corner of the house, until she heard him yell goodnight to Allie and Doc.

Today is as good a time as any, she thought, and none too soon.

She struck the match on the side of the box then stepped back and threw it onto the pile. There was a sudden roar as the fire caught and flames leaped higher than her head.

She watched the fire tear at the wood, the flames red and orange at first, then getting so hot in the middle of the pile that there wasn't a lot of color left, just a crackling, yellowish-white glow. Her back to the house, she reached into her apron pocket and took out an object that she pressed against her leg, covering it with her hand.

Her fingers played with the object, smoothing one side, then the other. Then, after a moment, she leaned slightly and flipped it into the hottest part of the fire. It arched upward, doubling in size, before it flattened on the glowing coals. For a moment it seemed untouched, then the edges began to smoke. Cora leaned closer, and saw Albert Junior's picture on the driver's license that lay under the layer of clear plastic. His mouth moved but she couldn't hear what he said.

She slid her hand into the pocket again, drawing out a dark Polaroid print of two unidentifiable women standing in a doorway, and a small, spiral notebook. Being very careful of her aim, she flipped the two objects into the hissing cauldron. They caught instantly; the photograph curled and buckled before it flashed into small pieces which floated upward, becoming lost in the maze of glowing leaves and wood.

The notebook, being thicker, took a minute or two longer. At first a few pages lifted from the top, curled and blackened. Then the searing heat caught the bottom, and the notebook exploded with a popping sound. The embers, crinkled and grey, danced upward and were lost.

Now the wallet began to burn. Soundlessly, Albert Junior's mouth moved again. Cora blinked and blinked at the tears running in the furrows that creased her face.

"You hid your real voice from Mr. Carl," she said, "but you couldn't hide it from me. Not after hearing it all these years. I thank the good Lord I was listening that day. I heard all those threats you made about Carly." Cora wiped at the tears with her apron, "She got elected to be mayor, anyway, thank God." Albert Junior's face grimaced, and was gone. Cora dried her face, straightened her apron.

"You hardly had to say anything that night, either." Cora's voice could not have been heard over the crackling fire, she spoke so softly. "You said my name like you did when you were a little boy. But, your mouth lied. It was like a round, black, lying hole in your face, then it was gone." She shook her head sadly. "It was your mischief that caused Mr. Carl to fall out in his driveway, and nobody there to help. I hope he can reach down from heaven to forgive you."

Cora wiped her palms on the apron. "God knows, I didn't want to do it, but I couldn't let you hurt all those good people." Cora waited, watching until the wallet turned into a charred, black ember.

A few of the publications of
THE NAIAD PRESS, INC.
P.O. Box 10543 • Tallahassee, Florida 32302
Phone (904) 539-5965
Mail orders welcome. Please include 15% postage.

THE DAUGHTERS OF ARTEMIS by Lauren Wright Douglas.
240 pp. Third Caitlin Reece mystery. ISBN 0-941483-95-9 $8.95

CLEARWATER by Catherine Ennis. 176 pp. Romantic secrets
of a small Louisiana town. ISBN 0-941483-65-7   8.95

THE HALLELUJAH MURDERS by Dorothy Tell. 176 pp.
Second Poppy Dillworth mystery. ISBN 0-941483-88-6   8.95

ZETA BASE by Judith Alguire. 208 pp. Lesbian triangle
on a future Earth. ISBN 0-941483-94-0   9.95

SECOND CHANCE by Jackie Calhoun. 256 pp. Contemporary
Lesbian lives and loves. ISBN 0-941483-93-2   9.95

MURDER BY TRADITION by Katherine V. Forrest. 288 pp.
A Kate Delafield Mystery. 4th in a series. ISBN 0-941483-89-4   18.95

BENEDICTION by Diane Salvatore. 272 pp. Striking,
contemporary romantic novel. ISBN 0-941483-90-8   9.95

CALLING RAIN by Karen Marie Christa Minns. 240 pp.
Spellbinding, erotic love story ISBN 0-941483-87-8   9.95

BLACK IRIS by Jeane Harris. 192 pp. Caroline's hidden past . . .
ISBN 0-941483-68-1   8.95

TOUCHWOOD by Karin Kallmaker. 240 pp. Loving, May/
December romance. ISBN 0-941483-76-2   8.95

BAYOU CITY SECRETS by Deborah Powell. 224 pp. A Hollis
Carpenter mystery. First in a series. ISBN 0-941483-91-6   8.95

COP OUT by Claire McNab. 208 pp. 4th Det. Insp. Carol Ashton
mystery. ISBN 0-941483-84-3   8.95

LODESTAR by Phyllis Horn. 224 pp. Romantic, fast-moving
adventure. ISBN 0-941483-83-5   8.95

THE BEVERLY MALIBU by Katherine V. Forrest. 288 pp. A
Kate Delafield Mystery. 3rd in a series. (HC) ISBN 0-941483-47-9   16.95
Paperback ISBN 0-941483-48-7   9.95

THAT OLD STUDEBAKER by Lee Lynch. 272 pp. Andy's affair
with Regina and her attachment to her beloved car.
ISBN 0-941483-82-7   9.95

PASSION'S LEGACY by Lori Paige. 224 pp. Sarah is swept into
the arms of Augusta Pym in this delightful historical romance.
ISBN 0-941483-81-9   8.95

THE PROVIDENCE FILE by Amanda Kyle Williams. 256 pp.
Second espionage thriller featuring lesbian agent Madison McGuire
ISBN 0-941483-92-4   8.95

I LEFT MY HEART by Jaye Maiman. 320 pp. A Robin Miller
Mystery. First in a series.   ISBN 0-941483-72-X   9.95

THE PRICE OF SALT by Patricia Highsmith (writing as Claire
Morgan). 288 pp. Classic lesbian novel, first issued in 1952 . . .
acknowledged by its author under her own, very famous, name.
ISBN 1-56280-003-5   8.95

SIDE BY SIDE by Isabel Miller. 256 pp. From beloved author of
Patience and Sarah.   ISBN 0-941483-77-0   8.95

SOUTHBOUND by Sheila Ortiz Taylor. 240 pp. Hilarious sequel
to *Faultline*.   ISBN 0-941483-78-9   8.95

STAYING POWER: LONG TERM LESBIAN COUPLES
by Susan E. Johnson. 352 pp. Joys of coupledom.
ISBN 0-941-483-75-4   12.95

SLICK by Camarin Grae. 304 pp. Exotic, erotic adventure.
ISBN 0-941483-74-6   9.95

NINTH LIFE by Lauren Wright Douglas. 256 pp. A Caitlin
Reece mystery. 2nd in a series.   ISBN 0-941483-50-9   8.95

PLAYERS by Robbi Sommers. 192 pp. Sizzling, erotic novel.
ISBN 0-941483-73-8   8.95

MURDER AT RED ROOK RANCH by Dorothy Tell. 224 pp.
First Poppy Dillworth adventure.   ISBN 0-941483-80-0   8.95

LESBIAN SURVIVAL MANUAL by Rhonda Dicksion.
112 pp. Cartoons!   ISBN 0-941483-71-1   8.95

A ROOM FULL OF WOMEN by Elisabeth Nonas. 256 pp.
Contemporary Lesbian lives.   ISBN 0-941483-69-X   8.95

MURDER IS RELATIVE by Karen Saum. 256 pp. The first
Brigid Donovan mystery.   ISBN 0-941483-70-3   8.95

PRIORITIES by Lynda Lyons 288 pp. Science fiction with
a twist.   ISBN 0-941483-66-5   8.95

THEME FOR DIVERSE INSTRUMENTS by Jane Rule. 208
pp. Powerful romantic lesbian stories.   ISBN 0-941483-63-0   8.95

LESBIAN QUERIES by Hertz & Ertman. 112 pp. The questions
you were too embarrassed to ask.   ISBN 0-941483-67-3   8.95

CLUB 12 by Amanda Kyle Williams. 288 pp. Espionage thriller
featuring a lesbian agent!   ISBN 0-941483-64-9   8.95

DEATH DOWN UNDER by Claire McNab. 240 pp. 3rd Det.
Insp. Carol Ashton mystery.   ISBN 0-941483-39-8   8.95

MONTANA FEATHERS by Penny Hayes. 256 pp. Vivian and
Elizabeth find love in frontier Montana.   ISBN 0-941483-61-4   8.95

CHESAPEAKE PROJECT by Phyllis Horn. 304 pp. Jessie & Meredith in perilous adventure. ISBN 0-941483-58-4   8.95

LIFESTYLES by Jackie Calhoun. 224 pp. Contemporary Lesbian lives and loves. ISBN 0-941483-57-6   8.95

VIRAGO by Karen Marie Christa Minns. 208 pp. Darsen has chosen Ginny. ISBN 0-941483-56-8   8.95

WILDERNESS TREK by Dorothy Tell. 192 pp. Six women on vacation learning "new" skills. ISBN 0-941483-60-6   8.95

MURDER BY THE BOOK by Pat Welch. 256 pp. A Helen Black Mystery. First in a series. ISBN 0-941483-59-2   8.95

BERRIGAN by Vicki P. McConnell. 176 pp. Youthful Lesbian — romantic, idealistic Berrigan. ISBN 0-941483-55-X   8.95

LESBIANS IN GERMANY by Lillian Faderman & B. Eriksson. 128 pp. Fiction, poetry, essays. ISBN 0-941483-62-2   8.95

THERE'S SOMETHING I'VE BEEN MEANING TO TELL YOU Ed. by Loralee MacPike. 288 pp. Gay men and lesbians coming out to their children. ISBN 0-941483-44-4   9.95
ISBN 0-941483-54-1   16.95

LIFTING BELLY by Gertrude Stein. Ed. by Rebecca Mark. 104 pp. Erotic poetry. ISBN 0-941483-51-7   8.95
ISBN 0-941483-53-3   14.95

ROSE PENSKI by Roz Perry. 192 pp. Adult lovers in a long-term relationship. ISBN 0-941483-37-1   8.95

AFTER THE FIRE by Jane Rule. 256 pp. Warm, human novel by this incomparable author. ISBN 0-941483-45-2   8.95

SUE SLATE, PRIVATE EYE by Lee Lynch. 176 pp. The gay folk of Peacock Alley are all cats. ISBN 0-941483-52-5   8.95

CHRIS by Randy Salem. 224 pp. Golden oldie. Handsome Chris and her adventures. ISBN 0-941483-42-8   8.95

THREE WOMEN by March Hastings. 232 pp. Golden oldie. A triangle among wealthy sophisticates. ISBN 0-941483-43-6   8.95

RICE AND BEANS by Valeria Taylor. 232 pp. Love and romance on poverty row. ISBN 0-941483-41-X   8.95

PLEASURES by Robbi Sommers. 204 pp. Unprecedented eroticism. ISBN 0-941483-49-5   8.95

EDGEWISE by Camarin Grae. 372 pp. Spellbinding adventure. ISBN 0-941483-19-3   9.95

FATAL REUNION by Claire McNab. 224 pp. 2nd Det. Inspec. Carol Ashton mystery. ISBN 0-941483-40-1   8.95

KEEP TO ME STRANGER by Sarah Aldridge. 372 pp. Romance set in a department store dynasty. ISBN 0-941483-38-X   9.95

HEARTSCAPE by Sue Gambill. 204 pp. American lesbian in
Portugal.   ISBN 0-941483-33-9   8.95

IN THE BLOOD by Lauren Wright Douglas. 252 pp. Lesbian
science fiction adventure fantasy   ISBN 0-941483-22-3   8.95

THE BEE'S KISS by Shirley Verel. 216 pp. Delicate, delicious
romance.   ISBN 0-941483-36-3   8.95

RAGING MOTHER MOUNTAIN by Pat Emmerson. 264 pp.
Furosa Firechild's adventures in Wonderland. ISBN 0-941483-35-5   8.95

IN EVERY PORT by Karin Kallmaker. 228 pp. Jessica's sexy,
adventuresome travels.   ISBN 0-941483-37-7   8.95

OF LOVE AND GLORY by Evelyn Kennedy. 192 pp. Exciting
WWII romance.   ISBN 0-941483-32-0   8.95

CLICKING STONES by Nancy Tyler Glenn. 288 pp. Love
transcending time.   ISBN 0-941483-31-2   9.95

SURVIVING SISTERS by Gail Pass. 252 pp. Powerful love
story.   ISBN 0-941483-16-9   8.95

SOUTH OF THE LINE by Catherine Ennis. 216 pp. Civil War
adventure.   ISBN 0-941483-29-0   8.95

WOMAN PLUS WOMAN by Dolores Klaich. 300 pp. Supurb
Lesbian overview.   ISBN 0-941483-28-2   9.95

SLOW DANCING AT MISS POLLY'S by Sheila Ortiz Taylor.
96 pp. Lesbian Poetry   ISBN 0-941483-30-4   7.95

DOUBLE DAUGHTER by Vicki P. McConnell. 216 pp. A Nyla
Wade Mystery, third in the series.   ISBN 0-941483-26-6   8.95

HEAVY GILT by Delores Klaich. 192 pp. Lesbian detective/
disappearing homophobes/upper class gay society.

                                   ISBN 0-941483-25-8   8.95

THE FINER GRAIN by Denise Ohio. 216 pp. Brilliant young
college lesbian novel.   ISBN 0-941483-11-8   8.95

THE AMAZON TRAIL by Lee Lynch. 216 pp. Life, travel & lore
of famous lesbian author.   ISBN 0-941483-27-4   8.95

HIGH CONTRAST by Jessie Lattimore. 264 pp. Women of the
Crystal Palace.   ISBN 0-941483-17-7   8.95

OCTOBER OBSESSION by Meredith More. Josie's rich, secret
Lesbian life.   ISBN 0-941483-18-5   8.95

LESBIAN CROSSROADS by Ruth Baetz. 276 pp. Contemporary
Lesbian lives.   ISBN 0-941483-21-5   9.95

BEFORE STONEWALL: THE MAKING OF A GAY AND
LESBIAN COMMUNITY by Andrea Weiss & Greta Schiller.
96 pp., 25 illus.   ISBN 0-941483-20-7   7.95

WE WALK THE BACK OF THE TIGER by Patricia A. Murphy.
192 pp. Romantic Lesbian novel/beginning women's movement.
ISBN 0-941483-13-4   8.95

SUNDAY'S CHILD by Joyce Bright. 216 pp. Lesbian athletics, at
last the novel about sports.   ISBN 0-941483-12-6   8.95

OSTEN'S BAY by Zenobia N. Vole. 204 pp. Sizzling adventure
romance set on Bonaire.   ISBN 0-941483-15-0   8.95

LESSONS IN MURDER by Claire McNab. 216 pp. 1st Det. Inspec.
Carol Ashton mystery — erotic tension!.   ISBN 0-941483-14-2   8.95

YELLOWTHROAT by Penny Hayes. 240 pp. Margarita, bandit,
kidnaps Julia.   ISBN 0-941483-10-X   8.95

SAPPHISTRY: THE BOOK OF LESBIAN SEXUALITY by
Pat Califia. 3d edition, revised. 208 pp.   ISBN 0-941483-24-X   8.95

CHERISHED LOVE by Evelyn Kennedy. 192 pp. Erotic
Lesbian love story.   ISBN 0-941483-08-8   8.95

LAST SEPTEMBER by Helen R. Hull. 208 pp. Six stories & a
glorious novella.   ISBN 0-941483-09-6   8.95

THE SECRET IN THE BIRD by Camarin Grae. 312 pp. Striking,
psychological suspense novel.   ISBN 0-941483-05-3   8.95

TO THE LIGHTNING by Catherine Ennis. 208 pp. Romantic
Lesbian 'Robinson Crusoe' adventure.   ISBN 0-941483-06-1   8.95

THE OTHER SIDE OF VENUS by Shirley Verel. 224 pp.
Luminous, romantic love story.   ISBN 0-941483-07-X   8.95

DREAMS AND SWORDS by Katherine V. Forrest. 192 pp.
Romantic, erotic, imaginative stories.   ISBN 0-941483-03-7   8.95

MEMORY BOARD by Jane Rule. 336 pp. Memorable novel
about an aging Lesbian couple.   ISBN 0-941483-02-9   9.95

THE ALWAYS ANONYMOUS BEAST by Lauren Wright
Douglas. 224 pp. A Caitlin Reece mystery. First in a series.
ISBN 0-941483-04-5   8.95

SEARCHING FOR SPRING by Patricia A. Murphy. 224 pp.
Novel about the recovery of love.   ISBN 0-941483-00-2   8.95

DUSTY'S QUEEN OF HEARTS DINER by Lee Lynch. 240 pp.
Romantic blue-collar novel.   ISBN 0-941483-01-0   8.95

PARENTS MATTER by Ann Muller. 240 pp. Parents'
relationships with Lesbian daughters and gay sons.
ISBN 0-930044-91-6   9.95

THE PEARLS by Shelley Smith. 176 pp. Passion and fun in
the Caribbean sun.   ISBN 0-930044-93-2   7.95

MAGDALENA by Sarah Aldridge. 352 pp. Epic Lesbian novel
set on three continents. ISBN 0-930044-99-1   8.95

THE BLACK AND WHITE OF IT by Ann Allen Shockley.
144 pp. Short stories. ISBN 0-930044-96-7   7.95

SAY JESUS AND COME TO ME by Ann Allen Shockley. 288
pp. Contemporary romance. ISBN 0-930044-98-3   8.95

LOVING HER by Ann Allen Shockley. 192 pp. Romantic love
story. ISBN 0-930044-97-5   7.95

MURDER AT THE NIGHTWOOD BAR by Katherine V.
Forrest. 240 pp. A Kate Delafield mystery. Second in a series.
ISBN 0-930044-92-4   8.95

ZOE'S BOOK by Gail Pass. 224 pp. Passionate, obsessive love
story. ISBN 0-930044-95-9   7.95

WINGED DANCER by Camarin Grae. 228 pp. Erotic Lesbian
adventure story. ISBN 0-930044-88-6   8.95

PAZ by Camarin Grae. 336 pp. Romantic Lesbian adventurer
with the power to change the world. ISBN 0-930044-89-4   8.95

SOUL SNATCHER by Camarin Grae. 224 pp. A puzzle, an
adventure, a mystery — Lesbian romance. ISBN 0-930044-90-8   8.95

THE LOVE OF GOOD WOMEN by Isabel Miller. 224 pp.
Long-awaited new novel by the author of the beloved *Patience
and Sarah.* ISBN 0-930044-81-9   8.95

THE HOUSE AT PELHAM FALLS by Brenda Weathers. 240
pp. Suspenseful Lesbian ghost story. ISBN 0-930044-79-7   7.95

HOME IN YOUR HANDS by Lee Lynch. 240 pp. More stories
from the author of *Old Dyke Tales.* ISBN 0-930044-80-0   7.95

EACH HAND A MAP by Anita Skeen. 112 pp. Real-life poems
that touch us all. ISBN 0-930044-82-7   6.95

SURPLUS by Sylvia Stevenson. 342 pp. A classic early Lesbian
novel. ISBN 0-930044-78-9   7.95

PEMBROKE PARK by Michelle Martin. 256 pp. Derring-do
and daring romance in Regency England. ISBN 0-930044-77-0   7.95

THE LONG TRAIL by Penny Hayes. 248 pp. Vivid adventures
of two women in love in the old west. ISBN 0-930044-76-2   8.95

HORIZON OF THE HEART by Shelley Smith. 192 pp. Hot
romance in summertime New England. ISBN 0-930044-75-4   7.95

AN EMERGENCE OF GREEN by Katherine V. Forrest. 288
pp. Powerful novel of sexual discovery. ISBN 0-930044-69-X   9.95

THE LESBIAN PERIODICALS INDEX edited by Claire
Potter. 432 pp. Author & subject index. ISBN 0-930044-74-6   29.95

DESERT OF THE HEART by Jane Rule. 224 pp. A classic;
basis for the movie *Desert Hearts*.   ISBN 0-930044-73-8   8.95

SPRING FORWARD/FALL BACK by Sheila Ortiz Taylor.
288 pp. Literary novel of timeless love.   ISBN 0-930044-70-3   7.95

FOR KEEPS by Elisabeth Nonas. 144 pp. Contemporary novel
about losing and finding love.   ISBN 0-930044-71-1   7.95

TORCHLIGHT TO VALHALLA by Gale Wilhelm. 128 pp.
Classic novel by a great Lesbian writer.   ISBN 0-930044-68-1   7.95

LESBIAN NUNS: BREAKING SILENCE edited by Rosemary
Curb and Nancy Manahan. 432 pp. Unprecedented autobiographies
of religious life.   ISBN 0-930044-62-2   9.95

THE SWASHBUCKLER by Lee Lynch. 288 pp. Colorful novel
set in Greenwich Village in the sixties.   ISBN 0-930044-66-5   8.95

MISFORTUNE'S FRIEND by Sarah Aldridge. 320 pp. Histori-
cal Lesbian novel set on two continents.   ISBN 0-930044-67-3   7.95

A STUDIO OF ONE'S OWN by Ann Stokes. Edited by
Dolores Klaich. 128 pp. Autobiography.   ISBN 0-930044-64-9   7.95

SEX VARIANT WOMEN IN LITERATURE by Jeannette
Howard Foster. 448 pp. Literary history.   ISBN 0-930044-65-7   8.95

A HOT-EYED MODERATE by Jane Rule. 252 pp. Hard-hitting
essays on gay life; writing; art.   ISBN 0-930044-57-6   7.95

INLAND PASSAGE AND OTHER STORIES by Jane Rule.
288 pp. Wide-ranging new collection.   ISBN 0-930044-56-8   7.95

WE TOO ARE DRIFTING by Gale Wilhelm. 128 pp. Timeless
Lesbian novel, a masterpiece.   ISBN 0-930044-61-4   6.95

AMATEUR CITY by Katherine V. Forrest. 224 pp. A Kate
Delafield mystery. First in a series.   ISBN 0-930044-55-X   8.95

THE SOPHIE HOROWITZ STORY by Sarah Schulman. 176
pp. Engaging novel of madcap intrigue.   ISBN 0-930044-54-1   7.95

THE BURNTON WIDOWS by Vickie P. McConnell. 272 pp. A
Nyla Wade mystery, second in the series.   ISBN 0-930044-52-5   7.95

OLD DYKE TALES by Lee Lynch. 224 pp. Extraordinary
stories of our diverse Lesbian lives.   ISBN 0-930044-51-7   8.95

DAUGHTERS OF A CORAL DAWN by Katherine V. Forrest.
240 pp. Novel set in a Lesbian new world.   ISBN 0-930044-50-9   8.95

AGAINST THE SEASON by Jane Rule. 224 pp. Luminous,
complex novel of interrelationships.   ISBN 0-930044-48-7   8.95

LOVERS IN THE PRESENT AFTERNOON by Kathleen
Fleming. 288 pp. A novel about recovery and growth.
                                    ISBN 0-930044-46-0   8.95

TOOTHPICK HOUSE by Lee Lynch. 264 pp. Love between
two Lesbians of different classes.   ISBN 0-930044-45-2   7.95

MADAME AURORA by Sarah Aldridge. 256 pp. Historical
novel featuring a charismatic "seer."   ISBN 0-930044-44-4   7.95

CURIOUS WINE by Katherine V. Forrest. 176 pp. Passionate
Lesbian love story, a best-seller.   ISBN 0-930044-43-6   8.95

BLACK LESBIAN IN WHITE AMERICA by Anita Cornwell.
141 pp. Stories, essays, autobiography.   ISBN 0-930044-41-X   7.95

CONTRACT WITH THE WORLD by Jane Rule. 340 pp.
Powerful, panoramic novel of gay life.   ISBN 0-930044-28-2   9.95

MRS. PORTER'S LETTER by Vicki P. McConnell. 224 pp.
The first Nyla Wade mystery.   ISBN 0-930044-29-0   7.95

TO THE CLEVELAND STATION by Carol Anne Douglas.
192 pp. Interracial Lesbian love story.   ISBN 0-930044-27-4   6.95

THE NESTING PLACE by Sarah Aldridge. 224 pp. A
three-woman triangle — love conquers all!   ISBN 0-930044-26-6   7.95

THIS IS NOT FOR YOU by Jane Rule. 284 pp. A letter to a
beloved is also an intricate novel.   ISBN 0-930044-25-8   8.95

FAULTLINE by Sheila Ortiz Taylor. 140 pp. Warm, funny,
literate story of a startling family.   ISBN 0-930044-24-X   6.95

ANNA'S COUNTRY by Elizabeth Lang. 208 pp. A woman
finds her Lesbian identity.   ISBN 0-930044-19-3   8.95

PRISM by Valerie Taylor. 158 pp. A love affair between two
women in their sixties.   ISBN 0-930044-18-5   6.95

THE MARQUISE AND THE NOVICE by Victoria Ramstetter.
108 pp. A Lesbian Gothic novel.   ISBN 0-930044-16-9   6.95

OUTLANDER by Jane Rule. 207 pp. Short stories and essays
by one of our finest writers.   ISBN 0-930044-17-7   8.95

ALL TRUE LOVERS by Sarah Aldridge. 292 pp. Romantic
novel set in the 1930s and 1940s.   ISBN 0-930044-10-X   8.95

A WOMAN APPEARED TO ME by Renee Vivien. 65 pp. A
classic; translated by Jeannette H. Foster. ISBN 0-930044-06-1   5.00

CYTHEREA'S BREATH by Sarah Aldridge. 240 pp. Romantic
novel about women's entrance into medicine.
                                             ISBN 0-930044-02-9   6.95

TOTTIE by Sarah Aldridge. 181 pp. Lesbian romance in the
turmoil of the sixties.   ISBN 0-930044-01-0   6.95

THE LATECOMER by Sarah Aldridge. 107 pp. A delicate love
story.   ISBN 0-930044-00-2   6.95